D1783772

# TRISTAN

## *Resistant Omegas 1*

## Joyee Flynn

**MENAGE AMOUR**

**Siren Publishing, Inc.**
www.SirenPublishing.com

**A SIREN PUBLISHING BOOK**
IMPRINT: Ménage Amour

TRISTAN
Copyright © 2011 by Joyee Flynn

ISBN-10: 1-61034-500-2
ISBN-13: 978-1-61034-500-2

First Printing: March 2011

Cover design by Jinger Heaston
All cover art and logo copyright © 2011 by Siren Publishing, Inc.

Printed in the U.S.A.

**PUBLISHER**
Siren Publishing, Inc.
www.SirenPublishing.com

# DEDICATION

To everyone who helped me come up with a name for the series. Thank you for the countless responses, suggestions, and input. I needed it to be perfect and y'all helped me get there!!

# TRISTAN

## *Resistant Omegas 1*

**JOYEE FLYNN**
**Copyright © 2011**

# Chapter 1

It was the evening of the full moon, and I was leaned over a bed in a strange woman's house while she fingered my hole. While that might sound like a good time to some men, it wasn't for me and for several reasons. One, I'm gay, so she just wasn't doing it for me. Two, she was less into it than I was. Three, she was stretching my virgin ass out for the Alpha to fuck me in front of the whole pack. Four, she was old enough to be my grandmother.

Odd much?

I think humans called them arranged marriages, but in the werewolf community, it was what happened to an Omega. My parents basically hit the lottery when they had me, and I turned out to be an Omega werewolf. Normal werewolves could choose their mates, either human women since there were no female werewolves. Or if they were gay like I was, they could mate to another werewolf.

But not Omegas. Oh no, we were pimped out by High Council law. No matter what, we entered into a contract with an Alpha. Which Alpha depended on who was the highest bidder. I was being sold to Alpha Jared Craven of the Denver pack. And Rachel, an elder woman of the pack, was one of the four women getting me ready for the contract ceremony.

Now ask me how much I wanted to lose my virginity in front of an entire pack of strangers. Hell, this wasn't even my birth pack. I grew up in the Green Bay pack in Wisconsin. My parents stuck me on a plane this morning with two suitcases filled with everything I owned. Rachel picked me up from the airport and had barely said two words to me. There were other women in the room with us who were helping me get ready like a bride on their wedding day and hadn't even told me their names.

The best part of all of this? After the Alpha was done with me, his Betas would fuck me as well. Because the contract really was with the inner circle of the pack and none of them would be my mates. Oh sure, I'd belong to the Alpha as if I was his mate, but he could still find a mate for himself. And the Betas, well, the same went for them.

"It's time, Tristan," Rachel said as she pushed a large butt plug into my hole, snapping me out of my depressing thoughts. It had extra lube in it that would coat my passage thoroughly so no one had to worry about slicking me up before fucking me. Like it wasn't bad enough that I was a twenty-one-year-old virgin and this was how I was going to lose my precious gift? No, they couldn't even be bothered with foreplay or stretching me themselves.

"Let's just get this over with," I grumbled as I put on the robe one of the women handed me. I followed Rachel out of the house as the other women flanked us. We loaded up into a large Dodge Durango along with a few men of the pack. Again, I didn't know any of their names, but why would anyone care to be polite to the Omega?

We were just a possession to be traded and sold according to werewolf law. We were a tool to help the inner circle grow in power and stabilize a pack. The more the Alpha and his Betas fucked me, the stronger they would become, and I would come into powers of my own that would help the pack.

As we drove to the Denver pack's hunting grounds, I stared out the window and cursed my existence. While it was great for my parents to have had an Omega for a child, it sucked being the Omega.

Hell, my parents could retire for the amount that was paid for me and never have to worry about money again. Did I see any of that? Fuck no.

And I didn't even get a mate of my own. I basically would spend my life being the fuck buddy of three men who could have mates of their own. Blinking rapidly, I tried to keep the tears that had threatened to fall all day. I was already small, so I didn't need to appear weak to my new pack. At five-five and a hundred and twenty-five pounds, I couldn't stop what was about to happen even if I knew how.

Werewolf law was that Omegas were contracted out to an Alpha. Any that were over the age of twenty-one and weren't *owned* by an Alpha would be considered rogue and put down. But we were rare enough where all packs and councils did everything in their power that some Alpha benefited from us.

The vehicle stopped, we all got out, and I was led to the middle of a large clearing. This had to be the ceremonial circle that every pack land had. It's where certain activities, like the claiming of a new pack Omega, would happen away from outsider eyes. The sun had set a few hours ago, and the moon was almost all the way up in the sky.

"Alpha Jared, your Omega has been prepared," Rachel announced loudly as we stopped in front of a large man. Guess this was my new master. He was gorgeous at least. That was one of my many fears about all of this, that I'd get stuck with some old guy who would touch me and make me want to vomit.

The Alpha was about six-three, two fifty with shoulder-length dark brown hair and very light brown eyes. He was built to say the least. I eyed him over as he stood before me in nothing but a pair of running shorts. His chest was nicely muscled, and I did like his ribbed stomach. There didn't seem to be an ounce of fat on the man.

"I thank the ladies of the pack for their care and guidance of our Omega," Jared said, the words scripted for the official ceremony. Another part of being an Omega was knowing every single tradition and role we would play. He bowed to each of the four women as they moved away from me and knelt by the other members of the pack who surround the circle. If I had to guess, I would say there were about seventy people present.

Great. That would make this so much easier.

"Disrobe my Omega," the Alpha said to the men who still stood on either side of me. I undid the belt of my robe, and they gently took it off of me, careful not to touch my skin. It was a grave offense for anyone other than the inner circle to touch an Omega.

Though I'd heard about Alpha's loaning out their Omegas to other members of the pack who were in their favor. That was the only thing my parents fought for in my contract. They seemed to draw the line at me being used by other members of my new pack. I guess three men fucking their son on a regular basis was fine, but add in a fourth and they would flip out.

I stood there naked as the Alpha's eyes ran over my body, and I fought the urge to cover up my bits and pieces. This was way worse than any nightmare I could ever have had about showing up to school and forgetting to get dressed. Mostly because I knew what came next.

"He meets my physical approval," Jared announced as he walked around me. Basically it meant that I was hot enough for him to want to fuck. I had several levels of his approval to win as the ceremony went on. I'd always found it amusing that if I'd been an ugly Omega that maybe I'd be saved this humiliation. Hell, when Alphas were bidding on my contract they received pictures of me and were allowed to ask my measurements.

Jared moved back in front of me and started to take off his shorts. Next would come the part of the ceremony where I proved that I would be able to be subservient to him and put his needs above my own. In other words, I wouldn't fight being his bitch for the rest of my life.

"I'm ready for my preparation," Jared announced when he was naked.

Since he was going to be fucking me, my job was to get him hard. I knelt down in front of him and opened my mouth. He held his semi-hard cock up to my mouth, and part of the ceremony was for me to lean forward and accept him. Which I did immediately.

His soft six inches turned into a hard and thick eight plus within seconds of being in my mouth. Part of me wanted to groan at the wonderful taste of the Alpha. The other part of me was very aware of the seventy sets of eyes watching me blowing the man.

I stared up at him with such hate for putting me in this position. Though I'd just be in the same spot with another Alpha if it wasn't Jared, I still hated it. He groaned and looked down to meet my gaze and did a double take. Jared schooled his features in a flash and looked away from me. I might have been on my knees sucking him off, being the perfect little Omega sub, but that didn't mean I'd lie on how I felt. Let him see how much I despised him.

"He meets my obsequious approval," Jared announced as he pulled out of my mouth. Basically I acted like enough of a submissive for him as he needed as Alpha. The tool for him to gain power couldn't be more dominant than the leader after all.

Next, two other men stepped forward, both already naked. I guessed that these were his Betas. They joined our little party now that I'd met the Alpha's first two requirements. As soon as Jared knelt behind me I leaned over so that I was on all fours. One of the other men knelt down in front of me as Jared pulled out the plug in my ass.

The Beta touched my cheek as he smiled down at me like a kid opening his new toy at Christmas. I opened for the six-five, two eighty muscled god in front of me and took his cock in my mouth as Jared pushed his way into my ass. While everyone has probably fantasized at two people wanting them, loving on them, this wasn't how the fantasy went in my head.

"I've waited years for this," Jared hissed as he bottomed out inside of me. There was a slight burning since it was my first time, but Rachel had prepared me well, so it wasn't bad. "You may receive, Cameron."

"As my Alpha wishes," the man with his cock in my mouth said. I guess his name was Cameron. Glad I got that before I was sucking his dick. He started moving in and out of my mouth as Jared started to fuck me. Basically Jared had formally given Cameron permission to share me and enjoy what I had to offer him.

I moaned as Jared picked up the pace. It wasn't that I was hard and turned on, but I wasn't soft either. And the nerves in my ass were feeling things I'd never felt before as a virgin. This wasn't bad. It just would have been a lot better if I'd gotten to know names, meet them, and basically say hi before we fucked in front of the pack.

"Fuck he's so tight," Jared said under his breath. He really wasn't supposed to say anything other than the ceremonial words, neither of them were. "He's even better than I imagined."

"His mouth is amazing," Cameron groaned. I knew the members of the pack wouldn't be able to make out what they were saying, probably chalking it up to incoherent noises or sounds of sex. They were all at least about fifteen yards away from us at the edge of the circle. "Shit, I've got to stop or I'm going to blow."

"Just pull out but stay in front of his mouth," Jared grunted as his thrusts became erratic. "I'm not going to last much longer. His ass is like heaven."

Cameron did as Jared had said as I felt more tears burn in my eyes. Everything in me was conflicted. My body loved that I was finally getting to experience great sex with a hot man. My mind was screaming that it wasn't right to do this in front of the pack with men I'd never met before. And my heart was breaking at the fact that they kept referring to me as if I wasn't right there being fucked. Jared leaned over and licked my neck as his sweaty chest rubbed over my back.

"He meets my primal approval," he announced and then sank his elongated canines into nape of my neck. It meant that he was feeling the need to mark me as his. Jared would mark me there while each Beta would bite one of my shoulders, once again showing Jared got the best spot to leave his mark on me.

I cried out at the pain of the bite, but seconds later it radiated out into intense pleasure. Jared lifted his head and roared out his release as he shot his seed deep into my ass. He pumped into me a few more times before most of his weight collapsed on my back. We both panted as he moved his hands to either side of me as he bent over me to hold up himself.

"He meets my sexual approval," Jared said loudly after a few more moments of catching his breath. Basically, I was a good enough lay to keep. That wasn't really what the ceremonial phrase meant, but in reality that's what he'd just announced to the pack.

I groaned as he moved and his cock slipped out of my ass. Jared knelt to the right of me as Cameron took his spot. The other Beta took Cameron's place as I never moved. This last man was about the same height as Cameron, maybe a little wider in the shoulders with an even bigger cock. Was that just a requirement to be in the inner circle of the pack? You had to be hung?

"You may receive, Rhyce," Jared said to the man in front of me. I glanced up, and this time it was me who was shocked. Rhyce was looking down at me with pity in his eyes as he held his cock out to me. I took it into my mouth, neither of us moving just yet.

"As my Alpha wishes," Rhyce replied, and I swore the man sounded as upset by all of this as I felt.

"You may partake, Cameron," the Alpha declared as I felt Cameron's cock push against my hole.

"As my Alpha wishes," Cameron said with a groan. He pushed into me gently, rocking his hips until he was all the way in me. They found a good rhythm together and after a few minutes Rhyce pulled out of my mouth before Cameron came.

He didn't move from his position, and I could see that his balls had drawn up against his body, signaling that he was close to his climax. His eyes never left mine, and he gently stroked my cheek the entire time. I wasn't sure what it all meant, but it gave me hope that maybe things weren't as cold as they seemed to be.

Cameron licked the side of my neck, and I shivered in response. He scraped his canines along my neck to give me warning before sinking them into the left side of me. Just like last time, I cried out from the pain that then turned into pleasure. Cameron came with a loud grunt as he filled my hole with his cum.

I started to get incredibly tired as he pulled out and moved to my left as Rhyce went to take his place. Then again I'm not sure how many virgins ever have back to back to back sex with three men.

"You may partake, Rhyce," Jared said once Rhyce was in place.

"As my Alpha wishes," he replied as he gently grabbed my hip as he pushed into me slowly.

It wasn't as if Jared or Cameron were rough with me, far from it. But the way Rhyce was handling me was as if I was fragile, or maybe even precious. I groaned as he bottomed out inside of me as he leaned over my back.

He didn't move for a few moments, letting me adjust to the new invasion of my body. And none of them were small men, but Rhyce definitely had the biggest cock, so I was glad he went last. He wrapped an arm around my chest as he nuzzled his face in my neck.

"I'm sorry this is how our first time together must be, my mate," Rhyce whispered in my ear. I gasped and instantly went hard at the word. "It won't always be like this, I swear it to you."

"Mate?" I asked, turning my head so that he could hear me while everyone else was oblivious that we were talking.

"I will take no other than you, Tristan," he answered as he started taking me slowly. "You may be our Omega, but I pledge myself to you as your mate if you will have me."

"Yes," I hissed as his cock grazed my sweet spot. "I give myself to you as your mate."

"Thank you, baby," Rhyce said as his body shuddered around me. He pulled me up against his chest as he went to his knees. I moaned as his other hand slid down my stomach, to my cock and started stroking me. "Come for me, Tristan."

"He's not allowed to come," Jared hissed so no one else could hear.

"It doesn't say that," Rhyce said quietly, but almost in a snarl. "It says we have to climax to make the ceremony official. Not that Tristan isn't allowed to come, too."

"Oh. Okay," Jared replied, looking almost shocked that Rhyce had thought of letting me enjoy this and have an orgasm my first time having sex. I glared at him with hate again, and the Alpha looked away from my gaze.

"Close your eyes, Tristan," Rhyce whispered in my ear, and I did as he said. "Ignore everyone else and everything. It's just you and me, baby. Let me please you. Come for me, my mate."

I felt myself getting close as he licked the right side of my neck. When his teeth grazed my neck I finally forgot the people who were watching us. I cried out even louder this time when he sunk his canines into me, shooting my load all over the ground. I'd never come so hard in my entire life. Rhyce went tense behind me before lifting his head and yelling out with his own orgasm.

He thrust into me several more times, drawing out my own orgasm as he filled me with his seed. When we were both spent and sated, we panted and tried to catch our breath as he held me tightly.

"He meets my inner circle's needs," Jared announced as he stood and stared down at me. Cameron stood as well while Rhyce pulled out of me.

"Thank you, Tristan," he whispered in my ear as he kissed the side of my neck. Jared kept shooting me scathing looks, and I glared right back at him. I knew why he was pissed. He was the big bad Alpha, but I'd come when I was with Rhyce and not him. I groaned as

Rhyce helped me stand and then moved away from me to stand on the other side of Jared.

All three of them howled loudly before shifting into wolves. All the other men of the pack joined in, and they ran off to hunt. It signaled the end of the ceremony and officially made me the Omega of the pack.

"Let's get you cleaned up," Rachel said as she handed me my robe. I knew it was part of the tradition that the same four women bathed me afterwards, but it wasn't a requirement.

"I can clean myself," I replied none too gently as I covered myself up. "Just take me to where ever I'm stuck living. I can shower myself."

"Fine." She shrugged and led the way back to the vehicle we arrived in. She didn't seem too broken up over the fact that her job was done, and I didn't blame her. I wouldn't want to be in her position either, though it was easier than the spot I was in.

My legs were shaky as I walked to the Durango and climbed in. I just wanted this night to end and crawl into bed. First, I would shower and eat something before I crashed. Part of the ritual was that I fasted for twenty-four hours before the Alpha claimed me. I never did find out why that was, probably to keep me weak and somewhat distracted as the ceremony happened. Either way, I was just glad it was over.

# Chapter 2

We drove for about twenty minutes before we pulled into the drive of a large, older looking mansion. It had gorgeous brick work with columns in front and a large porch. The grounds were extensive, and I could see a garden that had a gazebo off to the side. I guessed the house was on at least several acres of land.

I got out when the car stopped in the circular drive, and Rachel fell into step with me as I walked to the front door. It was already open, and a woman who was in her mid-forties stood there with a sympathetic smile on her face.

"This is Amanda, the head house keeper," Rachel informed me as she gave the other woman a nod.

"Thank you, Rachel," Amanda said as she moved so that I could pass her. I stepped into the foyer and wanted to let out an impressed whistle. The floors were a gorgeous white marble with a large stair case that led to either the second or third floor. Rachel didn't come in, and seconds later I heard the vehicle start back up and leave. "Let's get you settled in."

"That would be great, thank you, Amanda," I replied with a politeness I wasn't feeling. But none of this was Amanda's fault and I'd be seeing her daily, so it wouldn't be smart to make enemies. I might need this woman in the days ahead to keep what was left of my sanity.

"Are you hungry, Tristan? I could have the cook make something for you if you'd like," she asked as we headed up the stairs.

"I'm starved actually." I chuckled, glancing around to take in all the decorations. The artwork alone looked like originals instead of prints and seemed very expensive. "I don't want to bother the cook though, I mean, I can just make a sandwich or something."

"Nonsense," she replied with a dismissive wave. "That's what he gets paid for. And your bags are already in the Alpha's suite."

"The Alpha's suite?" I gasped, stopping mid step in the stars. "I have to share a room with him?"

"T-That was what Alpha Jared told us," Amanda stuttered, turning around to stare at me with wide eyes. "Is that not what was agreed upon? I mean you are his lover and all."

"Don't kid yourself, Amanda, I'm his boy toy," I snorted as we continued up to the third floor. "It's not in the contract that I will share his bed and room, just that I put out when he wants. I don't mean to put you in the middle of this or be a problem, but I want a room of my own. Can I just crash in one of the guest rooms for now? And I'll handle Alpha Jared later."

"Of course," she whispered as we turned right off the stairs and down a hallway. She had tears in her eyes as she darted a glance at me. "He's a good man, Tristan. I know all of this isn't ideal, pack law and all of that, but don't blame him for this. I can't even imagine what you're going through, and I won't even try to. But I've known Jared since he was a boy, and I love him like family."

"I understand," I sighed. There went any idea of having an ally in a house full of strangers. "I still want a space of my own, you know what I mean? I've just been uprooted from my home and experienced sex in a way no one ever should, and I'd like some place that was only mine."

"Let's put you in the room across the hall then," Amanda said gently as we stopped in front of a door. She opened it up, and we went inside. It was much bigger than my bedroom back home. This room had a nice king-size bed, desk, sofa, recliner, flat screen TV with cable box, DVD player, and even a mini-fridge. I saw a large closet and my own bathroom attached.

"This is wonderful, thank you." I smiled, feeling as if things were starting to go my way. "Can I just get my bags from his room?"

"Of course," she replied. We walked across the hall and went into his bedroom. She grabbed the suitcase on wheels while I moved my trunk and laptop case. Moments later we put my belongings on the bed and I went to check out the bathroom. It was sweet! I had my own garden tub with whirlpool jets and a separate shower. "Now, if you could have anything at all to eat, what would it be?"

"Oh, I'd *love* an omelet," I said, getting into the idea of allowing myself to be a little pampered. "Can I get one with cheese, bacon, green peppers, onions, and tomatoes? And maybe a side of sour cream?"

"That sounds excellent." She giggled as she gently placed her hand on my arm. I smiled at her as I took a moment to really look at her. She was maybe a couple of inches taller than me, and I realized she might be older than my earlier assessment. Amanda looked like she aged well, but the small lines around her eyes gave away that she might be mid-fifties. "I'll have it sent up in about a half an hour. That should give you time to get cleaned up and settled in."

"Thank you so much, Amanda," I said, hugging her suddenly as if she was my only friend in the world.

"You're quite welcome, Tristan," she replied as she hugged me back. "Every thing's going to be okay."

"I hope so," I whispered as we parted. "Is there anything I need to do? I mean, can I help with the chores?"

"No, we have staff on hand for that."

"Why do I feel like a pampered mistress?" I asked more of myself than of her. She gave me a weak smile as a response before leaving me alone. I didn't blame her, how did someone respond to a comment like that?

I ended up taking a bath when I realized I was sore in my ass, thighs, and knees from having sex on the ground with three men. It wasn't a bad pain, more like overworking muscles I didn't even know

I had. Then I started to unpack after I'd gotten dressed. Amanda showed up in the middle of me hanging clothes in the closet with my food.

She and I talked a bit while I inhaled my dinner. It was nice the way she was trying to get to know me, even if it was just my eating habits and favorite foods. I laughed when she promised to have my mini-fridge stocked in the morning with a supply of Mountain Dew and string cheese. That was what I lived off of most of the time, along with fruit.

When we were done, she took my tray with her and wished me a good night. I finished unpacking and stowing my suitcases before setting up my new desk the way I wanted it. Since I worked on websites for a living, I was kind of a tech dork. I didn't design graphics for the sites, more the coding, working with servers, and handling traffic on the sites. I'd worked hard and had several high profile clients that kept me busy.

Once I got the desk set and checked my email, it was almost midnight. I heard a commotion in the hallway and realized Jared was home. Seconds later the door to my room was thrown open, and I inadvertently jumped in shock.

"Why are you not in my bed? Get in my room immediately," he said with a growl. "Amanda told me some bullshit about how you wanted your own room. I won't have it. You're my Omega, and I want you in my bed."

"If you require my ass for your needs, I can be in your bed anytime you wish as stated in my contract," I replied coldly as I narrowed my eyes at him. "But nothing says that I have to share a room with you and sleep next to a stranger every night. There's more than enough space in this massive house for me to have my own room. I promise to make sure I'm always available for your inner circle's disposal."

Jared flinched as if I struck him as he took several deep breaths. "I guess if that's what you want, I don't have much of a choice, do I?"

"You are not seriously standing there talking to me about lack of choices in life, are you?" I asked as my jaw just about hit the desk. "If you think you have it so bad, you just let me know when you want to trade places, okay? I'll do what was promised on my behalf without my consent or input, but don't you dare ask more of me than that. You get to have a mate or fuck anyone you want while having guaranteed access to my ass, at least allow me my own room."

"I know this isn't what you'd have chosen for your life, Omega," he said with a snarl, letting me know exactly how unhappy he was. "But you might want to get to know me before you start assuming how badly I'm going to treat you. Just because it's in my contract that I can be with others doesn't mean I will be."

"Says the man who's never even said my name," I whispered and looked away when tears started to burn in my eyes.

"What are you talking about?"

"You just referred to me as Omega," I answered, looking back at him, letting my anger show on my face. "You didn't just say, Tristan or Tristan Modeto, you said Omega. So forgive me that I'm not thinking you'll treat me as a man when you refer to me as a possession."

He blinked at me several times before opening his mouth to speak. Instead, he shut it again, and then opened it again, looking like a gold fish. I sat there patiently while watching as the wheels working in his mind, almost able to see the smoke coming out of his ears. Finally he simply shook his head and left the room.

I burst out laughing after he left at the absurdity of the situation. Here I sat in a strange house fighting with my new Alpha, my new lover, over whether I could have my own room or not. My hysterical laughter was just starting to subside a few minutes later when there was a knock at the door.

"Come in," I said loudly, cringing internally that Jared and I were going to have another round of fighting. Instead, I saw Rhyce's gorgeous blond curls and deep green eyes as he poked his head in my room.

"Are you okay, Tristan?" He asked as he glanced around the room. "I wanted to see how you were settling in."

"I'm surviving," I answered as I stood and walked towards him. I waved him in, and he gave me a slight smile as he stepped into my room. "Jared's pissed he didn't come home to me waiting in his bed, but at least he caved and gave me my own room."

"If that's what you need to adjust to all of this, then that's what you need to do." Rhyce shrugged.

"Thank you for understanding," I said softly, feeling strangely uncomfortable that there was a man in my room. It was never allowed when I'd lived with my parents because part of the contracts Omegas had with Alphas was that we would be pure virgins and my parents wouldn't have gotten as much for me if my virtue was smeared.

"I was also wondering if maybe tomorrow you'd let me take you to a movie, show you around Denver since you're not from here."

"Like a date?" I asked, my eyebrows shooting up in surprise.

"Well, um, yeah, a date," he answered as he stared at his feet. "I know it's kind of backwards since we've already had sex, but I'd still like to court you like a mate if that's okay."

"Yes, I'd love that," I whispered as I took the last two steps to stand in front of him. "Will you kiss me?"

"You want me to?" Rhyce asked, his eyes darting to mine, and it was his turn to be shocked. "After what happened tonight I figured you'd never want any of us to ever touch you again."

"You were very kind to me and made sure I enjoyed it," I said shyly as I felt my cheeks burn up. "You want us to be real mates, Rhyce, and that's more than I could ever have hoped for when I was sent here. That is a big gamble for you to take since you have about as much choice in all of this as I do. So yes, I've never had a real kiss before and I'd like my first to be with you."

"You're amazing, Tristan." Rhyce reached out and cupped my cheek as he tilted my head up towards his. He leaned down slowly, giving me ample time to change my mind if I wanted to. But I didn't want to, I wanted to feel his lips on mine. It was better than I could ever have dreamed. The second his lips brushed against mine, I felt a jolt of desire through my body.

I moaned when he ran his tongue over my mouth, silently asking for more. Opening my mouth for him, I reached up and ran my hands over his muscular chest when his tongue slid over mine. He slowly explored my mouth as I melted into his very firm body, letting him feel my now hard cock against his leg.

"You're killing my resolve to go slowly with our physical relationship now that the ceremony is over," he said against my lips as his hands ran down my back to my ass. "I want to do this right, Tristan. I want to court you, move slowly, and eventually when you are ready, let you claim me as your mate."

"That's really what you want?" I asked, tears springing to my eyes. Alphas and Betas didn't normally want the mating marks on them. It was one of those stupid stereotypes that they were the big men, doing the claiming instead of being claimed. I was shocked that Rhyce would really let me mark him.

"Yes, Tristan. I mean it when I say that I want us to be mates, equals," he said softly. I smiled up at him as he moved his hand up to my face and wiped away a tear that escaped from my eyes. "From the moment I saw a picture of you last year and Jared said he'd entered into a contract with you, I knew I'd never want anyone else but you, baby. It wasn't just that you were hot, though I got hard just from that picture. It was the sadness in your eyes."

"What do you mean?"

"I instantly knew I'd do whatever I had to do to take away that sadness," Rhyce answered before giving me another quick kiss. "I want to make you happy, and that's what being mated is all about, wanting to take care of someone and wanting to love them."

"Thank you," I said as he gave me another soft kiss before stepping away. "And thank you for the most amazing first kiss in the history of kisses."

"I'm not sure I deserve the credit for that." He chuckled as he reached back and opened the door. "You were in on that kiss, too, and I can tell you that I've never had a kiss like that either. I think it was just the fact that the chemistry is there between us."

"Good thing, huh?" I winked at him before waggling my eyebrows. He laughed as he gave me a quick wave and left my room. I smiled at the door he'd just left through.

Maybe things wouldn't be so bad after all? Rhyce seemed awesome, and while Jared had seemed reluctant for me not to always share his bed, he did make the concession when he didn't have to as my Alpha. The fact that he hadn't played the Alpha card with me also gave me hope that we could at least be friends. If I had Rhyce as a mate with Jared and Cameron as friends with benefits that helped the pack, that was way better than how this could have turned out.

I turned off the lights and then climbed into bed with a feeling of peace I'd not had since I learned what would become of my life since I was an Omega when I turned fifteen. I'd always wondered why my parents didn't seem to love me as much as my older brothers and sisters. But when they'd sat me down and explained about pack laws and what being an Omega meant, I finally had some insight.

It wasn't necessarily that they never loved me. It was they'd always known I would leave. I think it really did hurt my mom that I'd be sold off like a possession and getting close to me would lead to more heartache when the day for me to be contracted off came. Either way it was a horrible position for me to be in, but the older I got, I saw that while my parents financially benefited from my contract, it wasn't something they wanted for their child.

Sleep came faster than I would have expected. I guess the stress, worry, and travel finally caught up to me as I fell into a dreamless slumber.

\* \* \* \*

I woke before the sun came up the next morning. While it was normal for me to only get about six or seven hours of sleep, I was still on Central time having lived in Wisconsin my whole life. Denver was in Mountain time, so it was only an hour later. But still, my body was used to getting up before five a.m. my time, so I woke up before six. I loved being up early in the morning. No one was awake normally, and I was able to get hours of work done before they did.

Ready to explore my new home, I hopped out of bed and used the washroom. Then I headed out of my room, and took a good look as I headed down the hallway and stairs. It really was a beautiful house. Most packs had an Alpha house that was older, bigger, like Jared's house that really belonged to the pack.

It took me a few wrong doors, but eventually I found the kitchen. I was grateful when I saw there was a fresh pot of coffee there and hoped that I wouldn't mess anyone up by having some. Though I was more of a latte drinker, regular coffee would work for my caffeine intake until I learned how this house ran and if I could get an espresso maker. I'd just poured myself a mug when I heard a throat clear.

"I see I'm not the only early riser anymore," Cameron said as he gazed at me from his seat at the kitchen table. "Good morning, Omega."

"Tristan. My fucking name is Tristan," I snarled before I'd even realized what I was doing. I was known for being a grump before I'd had my coffee, but Cameron didn't know that even if I figured he did now.

"I apologize, I meant no offense," Cameron replied as his eyes went wide, looking taken aback. "The only Omega I ever knew wanted everyone to address them with the respect of their title, not their name. If you prefer Tristan, that's fine, but I really didn't mean to upset you."

"Oh," I whispered feeling like a heel. Then I groaned as last night's conversation with Jared hit me. "Shit. I need to apologize to Jared. I've never known another Omega. To me, it seemed when people called me Omega instead of my name, it was a way to reaffirm my low status in the pack and remind me I was just a possession to be bought."

"I didn't mean it that way, Tristan," Jared said softly from behind me. I jumped, not having realized he'd joined us and spilled coffee all over my hand. "Fuck, I'm sorry, I just wanted to let you know I was here and not eavesdrop."

"No, it's fine, thank you for being considerate," I replied as I put down my mug and went to the sink. Jared was there turning on the cold water as he gently took my hand in his and ran it under the faucet. "A-And I'm sorry about last night. I shouldn't have assumed you were trying to put me in my place."

"I realized that's what you were trying to say after I left," he said as he turned off the water and handed me a towel. "I'm sorry I jumped all over you about not being in my room. It was rude and demanding, which was wrong of me. This is all new to me, too, you know? I guess I just assumed after we'd had sex you'd share my bed. But I realized that was a dickhead move on my part and didn't take your feelings into consideration."

"I'm glad you agreed to let me have my own room though," I replied trying to be nice. It was hard to focus on what I was saying as I felt the heat of his hand through the towel as he still didn't let go of it. "I-I just need my own space if that's okay? This isn't easy for me, and while you all have been much nicer to me than I was told to expect, I'm used to being alone."

"But you have family," Jared said slowly, his gaze darting to Cameron before looking back down at me. He picked up my coffee in his other hand as he led me over to the table. I was shocked when he pulled out my chair for me and waited until I sat down before taking his seat. His move of chivalry wasn't something I'd have expected, but I liked it.

"I think they kept me at a distance because they knew I'd be contracted to another pack one day," I whispered as I reached for the sugar. I couldn't talk to them about this and look at them at the same time. "I'm the baby of the family and my parents always seemed busy with my siblings, so I kind of grew up alone. I thought they just didn't like me until I was a little older and explained to me about being an Omega."

"That's rough," Cameron said as he passed me the cream and a spoon. I smiled at him as I took it from him. Then I doctored up my coffee how I liked and took a sip before saying anything.

"I'm kind of a bear before I've had my caffeine as you found out." I chuckled as the silence dragged out. "Sorry I snapped at you."

"Not a problem," he replied with a smirk. "I can take it. I'm just glad we ironed that out instead of letting it build up. We're going to just have to get to all know each other so no one's feelings get hurt by accident."

"Sounds good," I said before turning back to Jared. "I asked Amanda if there was anything I could do around the house to help, but she said there was a staff here that did everything. Is there something I can do to contribute to the pack?"

"You're the Omega, you're already doing it," he answered, looking confused, and I felt my anger boil back up. I took a few deep breathes before saying anything.

"I mean besides offering my ass up to the inner circle," I said calmly though I knew what I'd said showed my feelings on the subject. "Is there anything the pack needs that I could help with besides sex?"

"I know there are a few pack members that have their own businesses," Jared replied after a few moments, ignoring how I'd phrased my statement. "You could talk to them about maybe helping them with websites if you wanted."

"You know what I do?" I asked, staring at him as if he'd grown a second head. I was floored by the fact he knew I set up websites.

"It wasn't just that you're an Omega or hot that we wanted you to be part of our pack, Tristan," Jared answered firmly as he exchanged another look with Cameron. I darted my gaze between them as they seemed to have some type of silent conversation. "We weren't just looking for any Omega to help strengthen the pack. We wanted you. And we did our homework before bidding on your contract."

"The pack has put in a lot to get you here as our Omega," Cameron continued, turning to focus on me. "While having an Omega here helps stabilize and makes us stronger as a pack, it wouldn't have helped anyone to have an Omega that didn't fit in. We needed to know that you were someone that would work within the dynamics of the pack."

"Okay, whatever," I replied flippantly. It sounded good in theory, that they wanted me for more than a guaranteed piece of tail. But if they were so worried I'd fit in to their pack, wouldn't they have called to actually talk to me? You really could only learn so much about a person based on their resume.

"Good morning," Rhyce said brightly as he entered the kitchen with Amanda and another man that I assumed was the cook. I smiled at him, glad he was there and had interrupted the conversation before things went south. Standing up, I moved to meet him by the counter with the coffee pot.

"Good morning. Are you ready for our date tonight?" I asked hesitantly, worried he'd thought about it and would cancel.

"I'll be waiting for you at the front door at four with bells on," he answered as he leaned down. Rhyce paused as he was just inches from my face, and I realized he was letting me decide if we had a good morning kiss or not. I didn't even hesitate, tilting my neck and raising on my toes so our lips met. It was just as electric as the kiss was last night, and we didn't even use tongue. I really liked kissing him and planned to do it lots in the future.

"Where do you want to go eat?" I asked, panting a little from the desire I felt for him. I didn't move away from him and actually ran my hands up his chest to brace my weight against him. "Do you have a favorite restaurant?"

"I do, but you're the one that's new to Denver," he answered, slowly searching my face. "I thought maybe you'd like to do a little surfing on the web, and you could pick where you'd like to try for your first meal in a new city."

"Really? You'll let me pick?" I asked, getting even more excited to have a real date with someone who was so considerate. "I know there's a Bubba Gump Shrimp here, and I've always wanted to go there. Are you good with seafood?"

"I love seafood," Rhyce answered with a wink. "So we'll show you around and go there for dinner. Is there a movie you wanted to see?"

"Not really." I shrugged, running my hands over his chest as I started to get hard. "I'd really just like to spend time with you and get to know each other. We can't talk much in a movie. Maybe we could save the movie for another night unless there's something you wanted to catch?"

"Nope, just wanted to go out with you," he said before giving me another kiss. "Are you settling in okay? Is there anything you need that you've not found?"

"Any chance I missed an espresso machine or I could get one?" I asked, hoping he'd really wanted a true answer to his question.

"Why didn't you tell me you wanted espresso?" Jared growled from behind me. I glanced over my shoulder and saw both him and Cameron didn't look happy.

"You didn't ask," I answered, looking at him as if I was trying to say, "Duh."

"Look, Tristan, I know things didn't happen the way you would have liked last night," Cameron said firmly as he reached out and put his hand on Jared's forearm as if to keep him in his seat. "But it wasn't how we really wanted our first time with you to go either, okay? We were just as trapped by tradition as you were."

"That's nice of you to say," I replied as I turned to face them. I stared at them, wanting to believe the words, but not sure I did. I gestured to Rhyce over my shoulder. "But he was the one who showed me that he'd wanted it to go down differently, and you're just saying the words this morning."

"Is that why you're kissing Rhyce and not us?" Jared sneered, his upper lip curling.

"*Rhyce* came to my room last night, knocked, and checked on me," I answered as I narrowed my eyes at him. Jared's cheeks burned red with blush as any signs of anger left his face. "I asked him to kiss me. It was my first kiss, and I wanted it to be with him. You and Cameron might have been gentle with me and didn't treat me roughly. But Rhyce was the one who made sure I enjoyed it, wanted me to come, and asked me out on a real date."

"I wanted to give you space and figured you'd want to be left alone after what happened," Cameron said as his eyes darted between me and Jared. It seemed he didn't know about our Alpha barging into my room last night. "I didn't want you to think I was showing up for another round of sex or something when we got back at midnight."

"Well, I appreciate that you were trying to be considerate," I replied as my gaze shifted to him. "And it was thoughtful of you to have thought it out and tell me that's what you were thinking. But neither of you have said anything about wanting me as anything more than your Omega. Rhyce asked me to be his real mate. So yes, I'll kiss my mate whenever I want if he'll let me. It's not an attempt to punish you or piss you off."

"You're going to be his mate?" Jared asked Rhyce, his eyes going wide.

"If Tristan will have me," he answered as he wrapped his arms around me from behind. "I know I'll have to share him with you, and I'll deal with that, but I don't want anyone else for a mate. And I asked if I could court him as a mate even though we'd already had sex and I marked him. I didn't think that would be a problem."

"No, no it's not," Jared said softly as he blinked rapidly. I wasn't sure how to interpret the action, not really sure I cared. The fact that he seemed so shocked that Rhyce would want to be my mate felt like a knife in my heart. "As long as it won't affect our inner circle and Tristan's responsibilities as my Omega, it's fine."

"Don't worry, my ass is still yours to fuck whenever you want," I sneered as I stared daggers at him. Better Jared saw my anger at his words than the hurt I felt. "I know what my contract says, and the fact that someone wants me as their mate won't hurt your beloved pack or your sex life."

"Tristan, wait—," Jared started to say, but I ignored him as I moved out of Rhyce's arms and stormed out of the kitchen. It might have been childish, but I couldn't deal with him right then, and I'd be damned if he'd ruin my excitement over my date with Rhyce.

Once out of the kitchen, I raced up the stairs and back into my room. Again I thought of how glad I was to have a place of my own. The way Jared kept acting made me realize how I'd need my own room to retreat to with him in my life. As much as I wanted to break down and cry at the pain I was feeling from his shock that anyone would want to mate me, I couldn't let him affect me like that.

Instead, I powered up my laptop and got lost in my work. I ended up getting it all done and outlining a few services I'd be willing to provide to pack members for free. While I wouldn't do their entire website for no cost, I would give out consultations and some basics. Then I could give them a discounted price if they needed a whole site designed.

I figured since I was already giving up most of my freedom that they got in life since I was an Omega, I wouldn't act as a total doormat. Plus, I had most of the money I'd made hidden away in a few secret offshore accounts. From the moment I learned what being an Omega meant, I knew that I would need to have an escape plan in case things went bad for me with my contract.

There were places that didn't have any werewolf packs that I could escape to if I had the money. I'd already bought fake passports and IDs from a human that I had hidden away in case I ever was left with no other option. And I had no problem using them and disappearing one day if it became obvious that I would never be happy with the inner circle I was sold to.

# Chapter 3

Rhyce showed me around Denver for about two hours. He pointed out all the major attractions, stadiums, and his favorite spots. We had a blast, laughing and joking most of the time. I really liked spending time with Rhyce and was grateful he seemed to want me around. Denver was a gorgeous city with a lot to offer, and I was starting to be happy that I'd moved there.

We got to Bubba Gump Shrimp at about six in the evening, and the nice hostess sat us at a quiet booth in the back. After a few minutes glancing over the options, I realized something.

"I've never ordered alcohol before," I said quietly as I fidgeted with the menu.

"That's right, you just celebrated your twenty-first birthday!" Rhyce exclaimed, smiling widely. "Well, we're going to have to let you taste a few drinks then."

"Can you get something you like and maybe I could just try it?"

"Sure, but I think you should pick something out for yourself as well." He shrugged as he set his menu down. "It's not a big deal if you don't like it."

"Oh, okay," I said, hiding my smile at how sweet he was being to me. I ended up ordering a margarita, and Rhyce picked some import beer on draft. We told our waiter what we wanted and after he left, an awkward silence followed.

"Can I say something without risking the chance of ruining our amazing date?" Rhyce asked me as he reached across the table and took my hand in his.

"Okay."

"Jared and Cameron are both really good guys, Tristan," he said gently, holding my hand tighter when I went to pull away. "I know this is hard for you, being moved here, sold like a possession, and all around just being an Omega. But I think you might be letting some of your preconceived notions of how the inner circle treats an Omega cloud how you're seeing and reacting to them."

"Okay, I hear what you're saying, and I can see your point." I sighed. "But a lot of it I'm just going off my gut feeling as to how they treat me."

"There's always more to the story, baby," he said cryptically.

"What do you know, Rhyce?"

"It's not for me to tell you, they have to," he answered, giving me a sympathetic look. "I just know that they both really do have your best interests at heart and want to be with you. They might not be able to say it or even act like it after what they've been through. But I do know that if you let them in, we might all be able to be mates and be happy together."

"I'll think about what you've said," I whispered, ready to change the subject.

Rhyce took the hint and started telling me about how he'd grown up. It seemed he came from a big family like I did, but he was very close with his parents and siblings. He was the oldest of seven, and they were pack members.

I also found out that Rhyce, Jared, and Cameron had been friends since grammar school and had talked even back then about leading the pack. They thought they'd have to have a dominance fight, but five years ago the old Alpha was killed in a car accident, and the pack voted them in without any opposition. Which was extremely rare in werewolf politics and pack dynamics.

It made me think back to Rhyce's earlier words that Cameron and Jared were good men. To have seventy people all agree that you would be the best Alpha and Betas for their pack said a lot about them. Maybe I really was letting my bitterness at my lack of choices in life cloud my judgment? I mean, if I could be happy with where I was in life and who I was with, should I really care so much as to how I got there?

I found out after a couple of sips that I *really* liked margaritas. After having finished the first one before our meals arrived, I got a second one with dinner. Suddenly, I wasn't all that worried about Jared and Cameron. And I had a nice buzz as we finished at the restaurant, and Rhyce paid.

"Having fun with your first time being drunk?" Rhyce whispered in my ear as he guided me out the door as I went to turn the wrong way.

"Yes, yes I am." I giggled as he led us to his SUV. "And I'm getting really horny watching your fantastic ass."

"Good to know," he replied, his eyes shining with mischief as he started up the vehicle and drove us home. "So you like my ass?"

"I like everything about you so far, and not just the physical," I admitted, slapping my hand over my mouth after the words escaped.

"I feel the same way, baby," he said with a chuckle as he reached over and took my hand in his. It was less than five minutes until we were back at Jared's house, or my new home really. Rhyce parked the SUV and was at my door helping me get out before I'd even reached for the handle.

"Maybe you should carry me up to your room and have your way with me," I said as he wrapped an arm around my shoulders. He laughed as we headed into the house, up the stairs, and to my room. Rhyce stopped when we reached my door and then turned me to face him.

"How about we just have a kiss goodnight for now," he whispered as he leaned down. I moaned as his lips brushed mine, wrapping my arms around his neck to keep him to me. "I'm trying to be a gentleman, baby."

"But I'm horny," I whimpered playfully as he gave me another soft kiss.

"Well then I'm not sure if I showed up at the right time or if I'm interrupting," Jared said from behind me. I sighed and leaned my forehead against Rhyce's for a moment before turning to face our Alpha.

"Is this your way of saying you want my ass on a daily basis?" I asked, ignoring Rhyce's gasp of shock and Jared's scowl. "Fine, let me just say good night to my date and then I'll come to your room."

"If that's what you wish," Jared replied with a curt nod. He walked the few feet to his door, opened it, and walked inside without another word. I didn't miss the fact that he'd left the door open so that he could hear what was said between Rhyce and me.

"Give him a chance, baby," Rhyce whispered in my ear, giving me a kiss to the temple before turning and heading to his room. Cameron and Rhyce each had a room on either side of Jared's with connecting doors. It made sense since they were his protection, pack enforcers that they always had access to their Alpha if Jared needed them.

I took a few deep breaths before entering Jared's room, closing the door behind me. Glancing around, I didn't see him anywhere, but then strong arms encircled me from behind. I couldn't hold back the moan from my lips as he licked his mark on the nape of my neck. I'd never been so glad that I kept my white-blond hair shorter.

"Why does everything come out wrong when I try to talk to you, Tristan?" He asked, more to himself than to me. I felt his erection in the small of my back as he walked us over to the bed. "I want you so much, but I want you to want it, too."

It took me a couple of tries to understand what he meant in my buzzed state. Instead of giving him a verbal answer, I took one of his hands and led his hand to the front of my jeans so he could feel my hard on.

"But is that for me or because Rhyce was just kissing you?" He whispered in between placing soft kisses on my neck.

"I don't know," I answered honestly as he pulled of my shirt. "I had my first two margaritas."

"Happy birthday, baby," he said as he moved away for a second. I turned around and pretty much plopped on the bed when I saw he was already mostly naked. Jared was gorgeous, and any gay man would be hard at the sight of his naked body. Maybe even some straight ones. "Is it so horrible to be with me?"

I shook my head as he stepped out of his running pants. He took a step forward as I scooted back to the middle of the bed. Our hands met at the fly of my jeans as we glanced at each other.

"Let me, please. Let me make it good for you, Tristan."

"Okay," I whispered, letting him take over and leaning back on my elbows. He smiled widely at me as he undid my jeans and then pulled them down my body after taking off my shoes and socks. Jared ran his hands up my legs as he climbed on the bed, stopping when he reached my hips. I spread my legs as wide as I could to accommodate the size of his larger body. He leaned over me and went to kiss me, but I turned my head at the last second.

"I can make it just as good for you as Rhyce can," he said softly, and I fought the urge to cry when I realized it was hurt in his voice. "You'll let me in your ass, but not kiss you?"

"Kissing is the only thing I can have a choice about," I replied as he moved over to the nightstand and grabbed a bottle of lube. "I'm just not there yet with you. Part of me wants to be, Jared. The other part of me can't help feeling that I'm just a toy to you. And I'm not kissing you until I know for sure."

"I can be patient then." He nodded as he flipped open the cap and squirted a good amount of slick on his fingers. "I can show you that you're not a toy to me. I'll do what I have to do to prove that to you, baby."

I didn't say anything, simply moaned when he rubbed those fingers over my hole before pushing one in. I wasn't sure what to say. "I'll believe it when I see it" sounded like I was trying to pick a fight.

And just saying okay would be the same as I believed him, and I needed more time to know if that's how I felt.

"Is this okay?" he asked as he leaned over and licked my right nipple.

"Yes," I hissed as I pulled my knees up as far as I could to either side of my body. Jared moved his finger deep inside of me in circles, and I almost laughed at how different this felt compared to the preparation I'd had last night. But then all thoughts left my head as he rubbed over my sweet spot. "Oh sweet hell!"

"See? It can be really great between us if you just give me a chance," Jared said firmly as he kept torturing my nipple. I wasn't sure what I would have replied, but it became a cry of pleasure as he pushed a second finger into me. "I wanted so much to stretch you myself before I took your virginity last night. It seemed so cold to me that I didn't get any foreplay or time with you afterwards."

"Really?" I gasped, my eyes going wide as he scissored his fingers back and forth.

"Yeah, really," he answered as he gazed up at me, and I could see the truth in his eyes. "I need you, Tristan and not because you're an Omega."

"Okay," I panted, my head still fuzzy from the alcohol I had and his kind words. I just really wasn't sure what was going on, but I promised myself I would try to be more open with Jared in the future. I knew that I'd taken some of what he said negatively when it could have gone either way. And I was done with being that person.

"One more and you'll be ready," Jared said softly as he moved his head over to my other nipple. As soon as his lips latched on and he slid in a third finger into my ass, I went wild.

"Jared, please, Jared, I need," I begged, not having a clue of what I needed. I just knew that if I didn't come soon, I'd explode in a bad way.

"I've got you, baby, just let go," he whispered as I thrashed my head on the bed the faster he pumped his fingers in me. Seconds later

I felt wet heat on my cock as I realized he took me into his mouth. I lifted my head up, not wanting to miss my first blow job.

"Oh fuck, oh fuck, oh holy fuck," I chanted, feeling as if my eyes were going to roll back into my head. Jared smiled up at me around my dick as he swallowed me down all the way. That was exactly what I needed it seemed. My orgasm swarmed me like a speeding subway train. I screamed as I shot the first stream of my seed into his mouth.

Jared groaned loudly as he sucked on my cock, and I swear it set off another orgasm in the middle of the one I was having. I pulled my knees to my chest, my knuckles going white from how tightly I held them. Wave after wave of pleasure hit me as the evidence of it was swallowed down by my Alpha. Then it hit me as my climax started to subside.

"You don't give blow jobs to a toy, do you?" I panted, swallowing several times before I was able to speak. Jared stared at me as he pulled off my spent dick, licking the head one last time for good measure.

"No, no you don't," he answered as he pulled his fingers out of my ass. "Are you still not wanting this?"

"I never said I didn't want it," I replied as Jared lined up his big cock to my hole. "I just said I didn't have a choice in the matter and I wanted one."

"Did you just give me the green light or ask me to stop?" He asked, freezing his forward progression as his eyebrows drew together.

"Green."

"Okay good, because I think I'd die of blue balls if you denied me now," Jared sighed as he gently pushed into my ass. "We fit perfectly, Tristan."

I wanted to ask who he was trying to convince, me or himself. But I didn't. Instead, I rocked my hips as he worked his fat cock into me. We both moaned loudly as he bottomed out inside of me. Then he shocked me by leaning forward, wrapping my legs around his hips, and burying his face in my neck.

"Can I please, please, *please* at least kiss you here?" he begged, licking my neck and shoulder. "Please? I promise it will feel good."

"Yes," I hissed as he started to pull back out of me. Jared set a slow, gentle pace as he moved up onto his elbows and stared down at me. Each time he pushed back into me, he watched my face with his own look of concern. It took me several times to realize what he was looking for. "It doesn't hurt, Jared. It feels amazing."

"I just wanted to make sure." He smiled before thrusting in a little harder. "Is that still okay? Promise me you'll tell me if I'm hurting you."

"You fucked me into the ground yesterday, and it didn't hurt until later." I snickered, regretting my words when he turned his head as if I'd slapped him. "You weren't rough with me, Jared. It was simply that there were three of you back to back, and I was kneeling on pebbles and twigs. When I went to clean up, I realized I was kind of sore in certain places."

"But it's just you and me now. I can take care of you the way I want to this time." Jared winked as he started thrusting his hips faster. He nuzzled my neck as he nipped, licked, sucked, and kissed every inch of my throat and shoulders. "You feel so good in my arms, being with you is like heaven."

"Harder, I need you to take me harder, Jared," I whimpered as I threw my arms around his neck. This softer side to him and his intimate words were confusing me. I needed this to hurry up and be over or I'd end up crying while begging him to love me. But part of me wanted it to last forever it felt so wonderful. And I didn't just mean the sex. It was the attention he was giving me.

"Whatever my baby wants," he grunted as he pounded his hips into me. I hadn't realized he wasn't entering me fully before. The faster he went, the further he pushed his big cock into me. "I'm getting close, Tristan. Come for me again, I need you to come."

"Okay," I gasped as my body responded to his demand. I felt my balls draw up against my body as he put more weight against me. His firm abs rubbing against my cock set me off. I cried out his name as I filled the space between us with my release.

"Tristan," Jared roared out as his cock exploded in my ass. He held me even tighter as he shot stream after stream of his seed into me. I found myself holding onto him just as tightly as my orgasm started to ebb.

We both lay there for several minutes, panting while wrapped around each other. I was completely spent sexually after coming so hard twice in a short span of time. But I also needed to get away from Jared and process what had just happened.

"It can be so wonderful between us, baby," he whispered in my ear before rolling us to our sides. I groaned when his cock slipped from my hole, almost sad at the loss of our connection. Jared stared into my eyes as he brushed my hair back off my forehead. "I mean, you enjoyed that as much as I did, right? You came twice, and I know you weren't thinking about Rhyce."

"No, I was thinking about you," I said softly as I pulled away from him. Mentioning Rhyce's name confused me even more. Rhyce wanted to be my mate for real, so then why was I having these feelings for Jared too?

"Stay, stay with me tonight," Jared begged, mostly with his eyes as he held onto my wrist. "I'll clean us up, and we can sleep together, and cuddle all night."

"I can't," I replied gently as I pulled my arm away. "I need to think. I need to process what just happened between us. But I need to know one thing first, okay?"

"Anything, baby."

"Did you make it this intimate and earth-shattering because you wanted to or to prove that sex with you could be as good as with Rhyce?"

"I wanted to," he answered immediately, blinking rapidly at me again, and I still wasn't sure how to interpret that. "It's not a competition with Rhyce, that's not how I feel. But I do want you to give me a chance as you have him. I know I'm not the best with words, and every time I talk to you, I screw things up. So I just figured I could show you, if that makes sense?"

"I think so," I said as I got out of bed and reached for my clothes. I thought about how to say what I was feeling as I pulled on my jeans, but I just wasn't sure yet what I felt. When I had at least my pants on, I turned to glance at him, shocked by the tortured look on Jared's face. "I need time, Jared. I'm not saying no, okay? I was taught to expect being treated as a toy, and while I'm glad that's not the case, I'm kind of reeling from all that's going on."

"Okay," he nodded as he stood up and slowly leaned in to hug me. "I can't say I understand all of what you're going through, baby, because no one but you can. I just need you to know that I'm on your side. Whatever you need is fine with me, but please don't shut me out. I can't build a relationship with you if you won't let me in."

"That's more than fair," I said as we pulled apart. Going with my gut, I stood up on my toes and kissed his cheek before turning and fleeing the room. I really did need time to think about what happened and what was said. And I knew if I didn't leave now, the offer to sleep wrapped in his arms all night was too tempting for me to hold out against for very long.

When I got back to my room I stripped off my jeans, threw my clothes in the hamper, and took a hot shower. It wasn't that I was trying to scrub Jared off of me, more I needed the steam and heat to focus enough to think. I replayed everything in my head and came to several conclusions.

First, I'd not been fair to Jared and probably not even Cameron. Rhyce might have said right away that he wanted more from me, but they hadn't said they didn't want more from me. And while it had been my first time having sex in front of the pack, they still had to have sex in front of seventy people they *knew*. The pack members were strangers to me, but they'd known all three of them for a long time. That had to be awkward.

Second, that everything Jared was saying and mostly doing was showing me that I wasn't a toy to him. People don't get upset when a boy toy won't kiss them, or make sure the toy gets off. Hell, Jared got me off twice when he'd only had one orgasm. And he gave me a very enthusiastic blow job. Not that I'd ever had one before, but I think I could tell if someone wasn't into it.

Third, I needed to talk to Rhyce about what I was feeling. At first I'd been swarmed with guilt over my new feelings for Jared and that I'd enjoyed being with him. But from our earlier conversation, I'd gotten the impression he'd be okay with it. Not only okay with it, but might want all four of us to be mates.

And lastly, that Jared was being patient with me as he was trying to be more to me than an Alpha or use me as a toy. Sure, he'd had that outburst last night, but a lot of that was miscommunication. When I'd explained, he'd backed off and tonight, he could have pushed me but didn't. All the signs really were there for someone who wanted me, Tristan the man, and not just the available Omega.

I turned off the water, grabbed a towel, and dried off as I came up with a plan. I'd talk to Rhyce tomorrow morning and then once we came to an agreement, I'd sit down with Jared and Cameron. Though I thought it would be better if I talked to each of them one on one.

Feeling better about my new life, I brushed my teeth and got ready for bed. I had the towel around my hips as I shut down my laptop and then found some pajama pants. The knock at my door had me wondering if Rhyce had decided he didn't want to be a gentleman or if Jared didn't want to be patient anymore.

# Chapter 4

"Come in," I called out as I walked away from the desk and toward the door to my room. The one person I'd not been prepared for it to be stuck his head in before entering and closing the door behind him. Cameron. "Hey, what's up?"

"Jesus, you're like naked," he gasped as his eyes ran over me so intensely I could almost feel the caress. Before I could even think of a response, he closed the gap between us. His mouth came down on mine hard as he pulled me into his arms.

I was shocked at first, not knowing how to respond. But when he ran his tongue over my lips, I knew exactly what I wanted. I opened for him as he ran his tongue around the inside of my mouth. Moaning loudly, I threw my arms around his neck as he lifted me up off the ground. I wrapped my legs around his hips, loosing the towel in the process, but I was so focused on the tongue in my mouth I barely noticed.

"This isn't what I came here for, baby," Cameron panted when we broke for much needed air supply. "It's just you're so fucking gorgeous and you're half naked and all wet. I couldn't stop myself. I needed to kiss you more than I think I've ever needed anything in my life."

"It's okay, I didn't exactly say no." I snickered and then blushed when I realized I was naked in his arms while he was fully dressed. "I'm just not really sure what happens now. I feel kind of silly being the only one naked."

"I can fix that real quick," Cameron growled as he mashed his mouth back down to mine. I liked kissing him as much as I liked it with Rhyce, even though it was different. Rhyce was gentle and loving and sensuous and all about exploring each other. Cameron's kisses were full of need and lust and were maybe the most intense thing I'd ever experienced. He broke the kiss as we both gasped for air as he laid me back on my bed. I watched as he started stripping.

"Why did you come here?" I asked after I had a few moments of clarity to think. "You said it wasn't for this?"

"I came to ask you out," he answered, standing still as he held his shirt in his hands as if a barrier from my possible rejection. "I know I'm not Rhyce, and I'm a pretty big bonehead when it comes to feelings, but I like you. And not just because the sex was awesome, or at least it was on my end. I'm not really sure how to do this though because I've never been in a relationship."

"And then I was half naked and you attacked me instead?" I teased him, wiggling my eyebrows as I tried to lighten the mood as he fidgeted as if looking uncomfortable.

"Yeah, well, you're hot." Cameron shrugged finally looking up at my gaze. He smirked when he saw I was still making faces at him. "I know you and Rhyce are jumping right into being mates, but I'm not sure I can do that just yet, if that's okay? I thought maybe we could just hang out, date, or whatever the kids are calling it these days and go from there. I mean, if you wanted to that is."

"I like you, too," I said, figuring out how to reply to the rest of what he'd just said. "I think I need to talk to Rhyce before I agree to anything. I know he said he's cool with sharing me, but I don't think he necessarily knew you and Jared wanted me for more than a fuck buddy. And Rhyce is my mate after all, so I think it's only fair to get his input."

"Okay, that makes sense." He nodded after a few moments and dropped the shirt he was holding. I watched as pulled down his pajama pants to his thighs before stopping and glancing up at me. "But we can still have sex now, right? I mean that's where this was heading or if not, we could just rub off on each other. Or I like giving blow jobs, and maybe I should just stop talking now?"

"You're a nervous rambler, aren't you?" I giggled as I crooked my finger to come closer to me. He smiled widely as he finished getting naked before crawling onto the bed with me, his body between my legs. "I think it's endearing that you get nervous and ramble around me like that."

"I'm glad you think so. Normally people say it's really annoying," he whispered against my lips.

"I don't think that at all," I replied before giving him a quick kiss. "But I do have a request. Can we take this into your room? I don't have any lube in here, and I kind of want to keep my room as my sanctuary. If we play in here, then Jared or Rhyce will want to, and I've kinda said all around that my room is off-limits. That way no one will think I'm playing favorites."

"You had me at *no lube in here*." Cameron snickered as he picked me up and leapt off the bed. I giggled at his excitement and wrapped myself around him as I held on for the ride. It took only moments for him to haul me out of my room and down one room across the hall to his. "God, you feel perfect in my arms."

"Can I top?" I blurted out as we hit the bed together. Cameron froze as me moved above me so that he could glance down at me. I saw how wide his eyes were with fear, and it hit me what I'd said instead of what I'd meant to say. "Wait, I meant can I be on top. Like can I ride you? I've always wanted to do that. Though I'm really not sure why you look so scared that the idea of me inside of you instead of visa versa?"

"Scared wasn't what I was feeling at all, baby." He chuckled as he cupped my cheek with his hand. "Shocked. I was shocked that you would ask to top me when you've not initiated anything so far. I'm not against the idea of trying you topping me, but I've just never done it before. Everyone assumes with my size that I want to top so I have in the past."

"Something to discuss at another time then," I whispered as I lifted my head to kiss him. "But right now I just meant I want to ride you, if that's okay? I-I'm mostly stretched out already."

"And why would that be?" Cameron asked with a smirk as I felt my cheeks heating up. "Was someone playing with his ass in the shower?"

"No, I was cleaning up after being with Jared," I answered so quietly I barely heard myself speak. I couldn't even look at Cameron's face as I tried to move out from under him. I mean what better way to ruin the mood than say I just had sex with someone else?

"Hey, don't pull away from me, baby," Cameron said gently as he straddled my hips so that I was practically immobile. "I know that you're going to have sex with our inner circle. There's nothing wrong with that, okay? I've dealt with it, mostly because I think the idea of you with Jared or Rhyce is hot. And it's not like you said you were with Jared who's better in bed than I am or something."

"You're really not mad?" I asked, staring up at him, pleading with my eyes for him to really be okay with it.

"Oh yeah, especially if I get details or get to watch you guys go at it one day," he answered with such lust in his eyes that I shivered. "So now we were talking about you riding the bronco, right?"

"I was more hoping that you'd let me lead," I said, feeling my face heat up again. "I mean, how am I going to know how I like it unless I get a chance to play around?"

"Use me as your guinea pig whenever you want, baby." Cameron chuckled as he rolled us over so that I was straddling his hips. He reached up over his head to grab the lube from the night stand and then handed it to me. "Can I make a suggestion?"

"Sure."

"You might want to slick me up and see if you like a little pain with your pleasure," he said as he blushed. "I know you said that you're pretty much stretched out, but normally I'd still finger your hole and check. But I know when I've fingered myself I like a little burn sometimes. Just a thought if you wanted to play around and see what you like."

"Thank you," I whispered as I leaned down to kiss him. Cameron got what I wanted, the chance just to try new things and have some control. I moved my feet to either side of his hips and lifted myself up. Then I squirted a good amount of slick on his hard cock and rubbed it on him. He moaned loudly as he fisted the sheets.

"That's it, baby, get me ready for your tight ass," he groaned as I dropped the bottle on the bed. I smiled down at him as I lined him up with my hole and let him slide into me.

"Oh shit, you were right." I gasped as the slight burn radiated through my body. It wasn't something I'd like all the time, but I did like it. Taking a chance, I let my full weight go, impaling myself all the way on his thick shaft.

"Fuck, Tristan. You keep that up and I'm gonna come before we really get started."

"I really like the idea that I'm in charge of your orgasm," I said, smiling widely as I braced my hands on his chest. It might be silly, but I felt powerful at the idea that I could please big strong Cameron to the point of blowing his load. I swirled my hips around, making sure I was loose enough not to hurt myself.

"Tease," he hissed as I pinched his nipples.

"And you're loving it," I said as I lifted my hips up slowly before slamming them right back down. Cameron moaned loudly as he nodded his agreement. "Sit up."

"As you wish, master." Cameron snickered, but smiled to take the bite out of his comment. I groaned as the angle changed and I moved my hands up his chest to his shoulders. It gave me better leverage to lift myself back up. "Is this what you wanted, baby?"

"Yes, so fucking good," I moaned as I started to ride him faster. Cameron let me take the lead, but he did move his hands to my hips as if to guide me in my inexperience. I appreciated it since I knew what I was doing felt good to me, but I wanted him to enjoy it as well. Biting the bullet I decided just to ask. "This works for you, right? I mean, you like this and will come from what I'm doing?"

"Oh yeah, really soon," he panted as his grip on my hips tightened. "Can I show you something, baby?"

"Yes, please," I whimpered, loving the feeling of riding him, but somehow needing more. Cameron took me at my word and held onto my hips as he thrust up into me as he pulled me down to him. Oh sweet hell! If this is what he was talking about riding the bucking bronco, I'd just found my favorite position. The best part was each thrust up he hit my sweet spot right on. "I like, I like!"

"Come now, I can't hold out any longer," Cameron grunted as he pounded into me. I ran a finger over the slit of my cock, and it set off my orgasm. I screamed out his name as I shot my seed all over both of us. Cameron followed me right over, roaring out his release as he filled me with his cum. I liked that feeling, that part of him was spilling into me as if marking me from the inside out.

"I need a cowboy hat," I panted as I collapsed against him when we were both spent.

"What?" He chuckled as he kissed my neck, the side that had his mating mark.

"If I'm gonna be riding the bronco like that, and I think I'll be doing it a lot, I need a cowboy hat."

"Baby, we'll go get you one tomorrow if I get a repeat of the best sex of my life," Cameron replied than burst out laughing as he held me to him. "I've had good orgasms before and enjoyed sex, but damn, Tristan. That was something more than I've ever felt, like I'm a part of you now."

"I felt it, too," I whispered in his ear. And I had. It was as if I knew I would be forever bound to Cameron, and I couldn't stop the goofy grin that spread over my face at the idea. He might have been a big bad Beta, but Cameron was so much more than that.

I could very easily see myself falling in love with him, from the nervous rambling, to letting me take the lead during sex and guiding me when I needed it. And I was surprisingly okay with it. I just hoped he could fall for me as well, too, when I'd be sharing two other men's beds at the same time.

* * * *

I woke the next morning in my bed with another big smile on my face. As I stretched out the stiff muscles I had, I realized I could really get into this having great sex every day. While I knew hot sex was a good work out, I'd not gotten my normal run in on the full moon with the ceremony the other night. I got out of bed, used the washroom, and brushed my teeth before pulling on my running pants.

They seemed shorter than normal. I glanced down and saw they weren't hanging all over my sneakers, but barely grazing the tops of them. Not sure what to make of that, I shrugged and headed down stairs. Maybe they shrunk a little last time I washed them? But then they felt a little tight, too, and they were at least a size bigger than I normally wore.

"Someone has a present," Amanda said in a singsong voice as I entered the kitchen. I tilted my head to the side in question and she pointed over to the other counter.

"No shit!" I gasped when I saw a brand new, very expensive espresso machine plugged in. I glanced at her wide smile before focusing on the new addition to the kitchen.

It had a big red bow on it. I almost started to drool when I realized it was one of the machines where you just poured in the beans. It ground beans fresh, measured it out, and gave the perfect shot each time. And it had a temperature and setting knobs for the pitcher. So I could say I wanted three shots of espresso, pour milk in the attached pitcher, and tell it I wanted milk for a latte at a hundred and thirty degrees, all with the push of buttons.

"W-who got me this?" I asked as I ran my fingers over it reverently. "This is like an eight hundred dollar machine, Amanda."

"I don't know which of them did it, but they were all smiles when they left a little while ago." She snickered as she handed me a mug. "I was asked to make sure you saw it and enjoyed it this morning."

"Any chance there's a travel mug around here?" I giggled as I started playing with my present. "I didn't get a chance to go for a run the other night with the ceremony, and I thought I'd get one in before I started work today."

"Of course," Amanda answered as she went over to a different cabinet and pulled on out. "There are car keys hanging by the back laundry room on the way to the garage. They're all labeled, and I'm sure none of the boys would mind letting you borrow one of their cars. But you make sure to talk to them about getting insured on them before you use them after today, okay?"

"Yes, ma'am," I said, giving her a kiss on the cheek, and then started my coffee. "When you see any of them, can you tell them I went for a run on the pack grounds?"

"Surely, as long as you promise to eat something before you leave," she replied in a very motherly tone. "You're looking a little thinner than the other day. Are you not eating enough?"

"I don't feel thinner, my pants feel tighter actually," I snickered as my coffee finished up. It was a little warm for late January in Denver, so I opted for an iced latte today. "How about I grab an apple now and promise to have a three egg omelet with all the fixings when I get home?"

"Deal." Amanda laughed as I finished up with my new present and put the lid on my travel mug. I caught the apple she tossed me as she nodded towards the espresso machine. "Not such bad guys are they?"

"No, they're just not what I was told to expect, ya know? But I'm working through that and really trying to give each of them a chance," I answered as I suddenly found my shoes fascinating. "It's just really confusing, Amanda. I mean, Rhyce wants me as a mate. Jared and Cameron want more than just a boy toy, though I'm not really sure what. It's a lot to process and figure out. I mean, can a person even love three people?"

"I didn't say it would be easy, Tristan," she said with a sympathetic tone, giving me a half smile. "But I can tell you that I think there's no limit to how much love one heart can hold. I love my mate and all my children the same amount. Who says you can't fall in love with three men?"

"While I'm happy to have some choices that I didn't think I'd have, it would be nice to have a rule book sometimes," I joked, needing to leave before I poured out more of my heart to an almost stranger.

"Go run, it will clear your head and help you think," she said firmly, pointing to the back door that led to the laundry room. She really was a smart lady. I blew her a kiss before taking my escape. It seemed she knew I was getting uncomfortable with the topic and let me leave when I needed to instead of pushing me.

Making my way to the garage, I saw the hooks of keys. I choose Rhyce's SUV since I'd already been in it and knew he was least likely to be upset that I'd nabbed his vehicle without asking. And if he did get upset, Amanda gave me permission!

That last thought made me laugh as I pulled out of the garage, down the drive, and headed to the pack lands. I vaguely remembered the way that night, but just in case, I knew Rhyce's SUV had GPS. Picking the saved locations, I had turn by turn directions. Sometimes I really just loved technology.

Fifteen minutes or so later, I was pulling up into the deserted field by the forest. Really most pack lands were a privately-owned forest preserve. Normally they were held under some foundation name so too many questions weren't raised from the government or special interest groups. But then it wasn't open to the public like a regular forest preserve.

I threw the SUV into park, got out, stripped, and hid everything under the back wheel of the vehicle. Stretching out once more, I let the change flow over me, and moments later I was my small whitish blond wolf. It struck me as odd that I felt bigger than normal. How could I feel like I'd gained weight when Amanda said I was looking thinner than I did two days ago?

Shaking off the odd feeling, I started jogging towards the tree line. I darted around trees and chased a few rabbits while I thought about the past few days. My life was really turning out better than I could ever have hoped for already. And part of me was filled with hope that coming to Denver was the best thing that ever happened to me.

I'd been running about twenty minutes when I heard a few wolf howls. It seemed I wasn't the only one who needed to get a run in. I didn't feel very sociable at the moment, so I kept on my current path instead of heading toward the sound. But a few minutes later I heard another howl and realized it was much closer than the last ones. Maybe they smelled me and wanted to check out who was on their land?

Deciding it would be better to seem like friend instead of foe, I changed direction and headed toward the other wolves. It didn't take long until I found them. There were five wolves about fifty yards away. I gave up a quick howl so they'd see me. As a group they turned in my direction and growled.

That wasn't good.

They had to be pack if they were on these lands, so why didn't they know who I was? Every member had been at the ceremony, so they had to know there was an Omega in the pack now. Hell, we were the only white wolves! When they charged at me, I spun around and headed toward Rhyce's SUV. This wasn't a fight I could win if it came to that, and I didn't want it to go that far.

Unfortunately, they were much bigger and faster than I was. I'd just made it to the tree line when I felt teeth on my left flank. Seconds later another one tackled me to the ground and the momentum carried us into rolling several times before I ended up on my back. Deciding my best option was for them to really see me, I instantly shifted back to human form. The wolf on top of me shifted as well.

"Omega ass," he growled down at me as he pinned my wrists with one beefy hand over my head.

"You know who I am then," I gasped when I realized where this was going. They didn't think I was an intruder, they wanted to fuck me. And I wasn't sure they'd care if I wasn't willing. "Why are you doing this? I belong to Alpha Jared!"

"It's not just the inner circle that can get strength from fucking you." He smiled down at me, and I could see the crazy in his eyes. I struggled with everything I had, but the others had shifted and were helping the first guy hold me down. "And Jared's not here, is he?"

"Don't do this, it's a death offense," I begged as he moved his body in between my legs. I started to shift back, but someone slapped me hard and broke my concentration.

"Who do you think he'll believe if you tell?" The man sneered as he pushed my legs up. Another man held them when I fought as I tried desperately to not let them have access to my ass. "You're new here and just their whore. We've been part of this pack for generations, Omega. You'll keep quiet, and we'll work something out. I'm sure a slut like you would like to add five men to your list of who's fucking you."

"No!" I screamed as I reared up and head butted him in the nose. I knew it had been a good shot, but damn that hurt me, too. Just as I was about to be hit again, an even bigger black wolf tackled the man to the ground. Two more huge wolves went after the other four men as I scampered away to hide behind the nearest tree.

I heard the fighting more than I saw it as the stars flashing behind my eyes from the head butt finally cleared. Glancing around the tree I saw that the five men had shifted back and surrendered. And then I saw one of my rescuers. Jared.

"We couldn't help ourselves, Alpha Jared," the first man begged as he hung his head down submissively. "When we smelled the Omega, it was like I couldn't think past having him. We didn't come here looking for him, I swear to you."

"Leave now and I will decide later what to do with you all," Jared snarled as Cameron and Rhyce shifted back. The men nodded and ran back the way they came as fast as their legs could carry them. I stood up, clutching to the tree as I shook from the rush of adrenaline. Jared was the first to turn and look at me. "What the fuck were you thinking, Tristan?"

# Chapter 5

"Me?" I squeaked out, my eyes going wide. "How is this in any way my fault? I went for a run since I didn't get to the other night, and I heard howls getting close to me. I figured they smelled a strange wolf and went to identify myself. Next thing I know they're growling and chasing me! I shifted after he pinned me, thinking if he saw who I was, they knew I wouldn't be a threat—"

"You cannot be this fucking stupid!" Jared shouted at the top of his lungs and interrupted me. "They didn't think you were a threat, they wanted to fuck you."

"I kinda figured that out right before you showed up," I whispered as I felt my knees shake and want to give out. "I just don't get why. Why me? I mean, they had to know that I was yours, right?"

"Jared, he doesn't know," Rhyce gasped as he reached over and grabbed our Alpha's shoulder. Jared looked at him before his eyes turned back to me and they went wide.

"Know what?" I cried out as I glanced between the three of them. "This wasn't my fault! I didn't start this or do anything wrong, Jared, I swear to you."

"You're an Omega, baby," he said after taking a few calm breaths as if that should explain everything to me.

I saw tears shining in his eyes and while I was completely confused as to what was going on, I knew it was big. I closed the ten foot gap between us as fast as I could and launched myself into his arms. He gasped in surprise as I mashed my lips down to his. I wrapped myself around him as he kissed me with lips, tongue, and teeth as his hands supported my ass.

"Never again, baby. You're never to go out alone again, ever, Tristan," he said with a shaky voice as he buried his face in my neck. "We can't lose you, baby. And don't you dare think I mean that because you're the pack Omega. Fuck that, we can't lose you, Tristan."

"I'm sorry, Jared," I whispered as I licked his neck up to his ear. I still had no idea why he was so upset but I just knew I wanted to fix it. And after he, Cameron, and Rhyce just saved me from a possible fate worse than death, I needed to feel my big strong men. "It's okay, Jared, I'm okay, I swear I am. I'm just a little shaken up, but I'm not going anywhere."

"It is *not* okay, Tristan," he growled as he nipped my shoulder as his hands squeezed my ass. "We could have lost you because no one told you something so important like that everyone will constantly want to fuck you and your scent can drive them crazy. We could have lost you because I was neglectful and didn't go over the rules about you going anywhere alone."

"But you didn't. I'm right here and I need you right now," I moaned as I rubbed my hard cock against his stomach as I licked and sucked every inch of skin I had access to. "We will talk later, and you'll explain everything to me, tell me the rules, tie me to your bed if you want. Just take me now, Jared. I need my men."

"I'm not going to fuck you after you were attacked and almost raped, baby," he said firmly, but I felt his cock get hard and brush my ass. It seem his two heads were fighting as to who was in charge right then. Personally, I wanted the lower head to win. I moved my hips so that he was pushing against my hole as I tried to take him inside of me. "Tristan, you have to stop that. You're not even stretched."

"Don't care," I panted and then whimpered when he lifted me up higher on his body. I leaned back enough so I could stare into his eyes and see the conflicting emotions on his face. "Didn't I kind of make it clear what I needed when I kissed you? I'm begging you to take me, to feel you even if it will hurt because we don't have lube. Please don't deny me, Jared."

"Okay, baby, if that's what you need because I need to feel you, too," he replied, and I saw that lust had won out against everything else as he kissed me. "Get him ready."

I wasn't sure who he was talking to as his tongue slid back into my mouth. But I figured it out when I felt two more hands on my ass and then another set of lips on my shoulders. I moaned loudly, though the sound was swallowed into Jared as he never stopped kissing me. Then I felt someone's tongue lick my hole, and I broke the kiss to cry out.

"Holy mother of hell," I whimpered as I glanced over my shoulder. Rhyce's lips met mine, and I knew he was the one who'd been kissing my shoulders, and that meant Cameron was the one licking my ass. I'd need to remember to thank him later for another first time experience that I loved. "Shit, Cameron, I'm going to become your love slave with that tongue."

"Anything our baby wants." Cameron chuckled before thrusting his tongue deep into me. I realized Jared was growling softly as I felt the vibrations in his chest. Turning back to him, I saw the scowl on his face.

"Don't start," I ordered, raising an eyebrow as I tried to think coherently with what Cameron was doing to me. "I came to you first, begged you to take me, and kissed you immediately. Don't start this jealous shit because I'm complimenting Cameron as he's giving me pleasure and eating my ass."

"You're right, I'm sorry," Jared said as he gently licked my bottom lip. It was a sign of submission and asking for forgiveness in wolf culture. It was also something that werewolves did at times, though I would never have guessed in a million years that an Alpha would do it to his Omega. "I've just got all this adrenaline flowing through me, and you were almost taken from me, I'm feeling very territorial."

"We all are, Jared," Rhyce said from behind me. "We were both growling when he went to you and not us."

"I'm sorry," I whispered, feeling guilty that I'd upset them and totally missed it. "I saw how upset Jared was, and while I'm still not sure what all happened, I just wanted to make him feel better."

"Nothing to be sorry for, baby," Rhyce replied as he nuzzled one side of my neck while Jared did the other. Cameron's tongue was still busy, but he'd added two fingers, getting a loud groan from me. Three men were giving me their full attention as they each wanted mine. It was like I'd died and gone to heaven. "We understand it wasn't about you caring for Jared more than us. It was the situation, him already talking to you, and him sending the bad guys away."

"But you all saved me, and I know that," I said as I tilted my head to get his lips again. "I just needed to make his sadness go away. And need to feel all three of you, don't doubt that. I plan on having all three of you before we leave here."

"Then get on with it because you're ready," Cameron growled as he pulled his fingers from my ass. Before I could even say anything, Jared moved his hands to grab his cock and lower me onto him. I was more than stretched, but spit wasn't the best lube, so there was some burning. Which worked out since I'd found out that I like some burn last night.

"Take me, claim me, own me," I panted as I stared at Jared as he bottomed out inside of me. His eyes went wide as I seemed to say exactly what he felt right then and wanted from me. I wasn't sure how I knew that was in his head. I just did. "I give myself to you freely, Jared. No contract, no agreement as Alpha and Omega. I, Tristan Modeto, want you, Jared Craven, to own my body, my soul, and my heart."

"I accept and give you the same, baby," he said softly as one tear escaped his eyes. Then our lips met, and it was all fireworks and need. He moved us so that I was half leaning back against Rhyce and Cameron as Jared pounded into me hard and fast. I had one arm looped around Jared's neck and one reaching back around Cameron's. Rhyce held most of my weight up under my ass as he sucked and nibbled on his mating mark.

"I'm coming," I cried out only minutes after Jared had entered me. All the sensations, emotions, and need circling us were too much for me to handle. I screamed out to the heavens as I painted Jared's chest with my cum. My ass clamped down on Jared's cock, taking him with me. He roared out as he shot his release inside of me.

"My turn," Cameron growled as he leaned me back against Jared's chest and maneuvered Jared back against the tree. I'd just finished my orgasm, and Jared shot his last stream inside of me as he nodded to Cameron. I'm not really sure who did what, but I felt Jared's dick leave me and Cameron's pushing against my hole. "I pledge myself to you, baby. If you'll have me, all I want is you, Jared, and Rhyce."

"Yes," I hissed, and he thrust up into me hard. "Fuck, yes, Cameron. Pound into my ass."

"Dirty Omega," Jared panted as he leaned down to lick my shoulder. He moved a little, and I saw he was staring at Cameron. "You really want all of us?"

"Yeah, I want the four of us to be mates and a family," he grunted as he pushed back into me. "I've loved you and Rhyce all my life."

Jared did that rapid blinking again before reaching past me, grabbing Cameron's neck, and pulling him closer so that I was completely sandwiched between them. I didn't so much see as hear them kissing as I moved my hips on Cameron's cock.

"Come here, my mate," I panted as I caught Rhyce's gaze and pursed my lips for him. He smiled widely before his mouth latched onto mine. I gasped when Cameron started to fuck me hard. Breaking my kiss from Rhyce, I saw Jared and Cameron had stopped as well.

"I always knew you were what we needed," Jared whispered cryptically as he cupped my cheek. I wasn't sure what the hell he was talking about again, but I was so into the cock pounding into my ass I didn't have any brain cells left to think with. "Bite me, baby. Mark me as yours, Tristan."

"Really?" I asked, his words getting through my lust-filled haze. I felt my canines extend at the demand, but I needed to make sure. Jared smiled and nodded as he tilted his neck to give me better access. I didn't even hesitate. I leaned forward and bit him as he reached up and held my head to his neck. The second his sweet blood ran across my tongue, I grunted and came all over him again.

"Shit, shit, gonna come," Cameron cried out seconds before shooting in my ass. I lifted my head up from Jared's shoulder than and leaned my weight onto Cameron as he kept pumping more and more of his seed into me.

"I love these marathons when no one's watching," I moaned as Cameron pulled out of me moments later.

"Does that mean you still have some energy left for me?" Rhyce asked quietly.

"Of course," I smiled widely at him, knowing he needed some reassurance I wanted him after I'd just had my brains fucked out by his friends. "Always have more than enough desire for you, my mate."

"Good," he growled as he pulled me out of Jared's arms. We sank down to the ground as Rhyce lay down on his back so I straddled his hips. "Too bad we don't have a cowboy hat for you, baby, because you're gonna ride me while I fuck you good."

"You gossip." I snickered as I tried to shoot Cameron a scathing look, but failed miserably. I turned back to Rhyce and leaned forward on his chest as he moved his cock to my hole. "Brand me with that massive cock, my mate."

"Oh yeah," Rhyce moaned as he thrust up hard into me. I cried out in pleasure as he bottomed out inside of me. Bracing my hands on his pecs, he positioned his feet so he could get some leverage. He was good to his word, fucking me like an animal as I moved my hips down to meet him. "Shit, baby. I'm not going to last after watching you all go at it. You feel too fucking good!"

"Harder, Rhyce, take me harder," I whimpered as his eyes went wide. "You won't hurt me, my mate. I need to feel you for days after this."

"So hot," he hissed as he pounded into me harder than I'd ever thought possible. Rhyce pegged my prostate each time, and it didn't take long for me to not only get hard but ready to explode again. "Come for me, my love, my mate."

"Rhyce," I screamed as I shot my seed all over his chest. He yelled out my name and came inside of me as my body started to go limp. Lights burst behind my eyes as the force of my orgasm washed over me in waves. I was starting to get light-headed after the exhortation of coming three times in such a short period. But I was so glad I did since I knew it would hurt them if I'd come with one or two of them and not all of them.

"We've got you, baby. Rest now," Rhyce whispered gently as I collapsed on his chest. I wanted to say thank you and how good it was, but nothing came out. Vaguely I heard them talking in the background but only caught a few things.

"Is he taller?" Cameron asked.

"I swear he's heavier than the other night," Rhyce said, and that was the last thing I heard before the darkness took me. Glad to know that they thought so, too, or if we were losing our minds, at least it was all of us.

* * * *

"His file said he was five-five," Jared said, waking me up as I lay on something hard. I realized I was on the kitchen table as Jared, Rhyce, Cameron, and Amanda were all around me. And they were measuring me! I felt sewing measuring tape wrap around my hips. "He's 31 waist now, too."

"Really? You had to do this on the table instead of a soft bed?" I grunted, my throat dry from all the screaming earlier. Just that thought had me smiling.

"Shit, sorry, baby," Rhyce said as he picked me up into his arms. I smiled up at him, loving that he instantly took care of my needs. "Can we get you anything?"

"About a gallon of coffee and I could eat a cow," I answered as I tilted my head up to kiss him. "And yes, I'm five-five with a twenty-eight inch waist."

"Not anymore, Tristan," Amanda said softly and then headed over to my new espresso machine.

"What do you mean, *not anymore*?" I asked, feeling a pit form in my stomach as I got scared. "People don't have growth spurts at twenty-one."

"We measured you six times, baby," Rhyce answered as he sat down on one of the chairs with me in his lap. "You're five-eight and your waist is now thirty-one."

"You must have measured wrong," I said, shaking my head as my eyebrows drew together.

"We didn't," Jared replied as he sat down in the chair next to us. He turned it so he was facing me, and he eyed me over with concern. "You've grown, and we're not sure why. That's why Amanda thought you've lost weight it's distributed differently now."

"How is that even possible?" I asked, glancing from him to Cameron and then over to Amanda, who was making me a latte. That had another question coming out of me. "And who do I have to thank for my wonderful present?"

"Jared," Cameron and Rhyce both said as the man in question blushed, the tips of his ears turning red.

"Well, it's from all of us really, a belated birthday present." He shrugged as he twisted his hands together. I patted Rhyce's arm that was holding me to him and got off his lap.

"Hey now," I squeaked as he pinched my ass.

"Just checking that it hasn't lost weight," Rhyce said holding up his hands in surrender. "I'm partial to your bubble butt and needed to check it wasn't going flat."

"Oh, well then let me give you a better look." I smirked as I braced my hands on Jared's thighs and bent over. "Still bubbly enough for you, my mate?"

"Can I check, too?" Cameron groaned, and I felt his hands on my ass as Rhyce rubbed my butt. "Feels perfect to me."

"Glad you think so," I said, biting my lip to keep my own moan in. I stood up and then promptly straddled Jared's lap as I took his face in my hands. He finally met my gaze as I smiled widely at him. "I love my present. It's the most thoughtful, loving, wonderful present I've ever gotten in my entire life, Jared. It's way too expensive, but I won't tell you to get me something less costly when you obviously put thought into it."

"You're worth it to me," he whispered, and his cheeks got even redder. "I want you to be happy and if espresso makes you smile in the morning, I want that. If you want special coffee, we can order it, Tristan. I mean it when I say I want you here and we can't lose you."

"I believe you," I said, licking his lower lip. Jared's eyes went wide at the gesture of submission and trust. I didn't really have anything to apologize for, but in wolf culture it could mean any and all of those things. He growled his approval before mashing his lips down on mine. After a few moments of intense nipping, biting, and show of dominance in the kiss, he started to be gentle. "You can go all Alpha on me any day, it's hot."

"Glad you think so," Jared panted as he started to smile. "But if we went much further, I wouldn't be measuring your height on this table as much as how much force the table can take."

"Or we could see what else might have gotten bigger on me." I waggled my eyebrows at me as Jared's mouth dropped open at my innuendo. "But seriously, I love my gift. Thank you very much."

"Glad that's settled, and maybe you boys can remember I'm here." Amanda cleared her throat as she brought over a latte for me. "I left the heat setting where you had it even if you didn't use it this morning."

"You're a goddess." I moaned after taking a sip. I glanced over as the cook came into the kitchen. Amanda had told me his name was Frank. He was a shorter man, maybe about my height. Frank was always smiling, showing his wrinkles around his mouth and eyes. If I had to guess, I'd say he was about late fifties. "You didn't have to page Frank, I can get myself food."

"Nonsense," Frank scoffed as he waved his hand at me. "I like your style in the food you request. Something different from the constant steak and burgers from the other three."

"What do you eat that's so odd, baby?" Cameron asked as he glanced from me to Frank. "Not anything that could make you grow three inches."

"Frank makes the world's best omelet," I answered, batting my lashes at the cook. "I would be willing to give my left nut for a couple right now. Any chance you need some computer work done, Frank? I'll be your tech slave for life."

"Actually yes, my wife's laptop is being a beast." Frank chuckled as he started cracking eggs. Then he held up a whisk and waved it in my direction. "I gladly let you help with that, but you keep your nuts where they belong, young man."

"I agree wholeheartedly," Jared whispered in my ear as his hand moved between my legs.

"I could really get used to all this attention and spoiling." I groaned, leaning back against the table while drinking my coffee to give him better access.

"I picked up some fresh chives from the store. Feeling adventurous, Tristan?" Frank asked, giving me a wink.

"Oh yeah," I moaned, licking my lips. "That sounds fantastic."

"You really are sex on a stick," Jared whispered as he leaned over and licked my neck. I felt him get hard under me and squirmed in his lap. Rhyce and Cameron sniffed the air before groaning, smelling our desire. "Who knew food would get you so wound up?"

"Well, I seem to be a growing boy." I smirked but then felt cold. We still didn't know why I was growing, and it was kind of scary.

"I swear I'm going to get a bucket of ice for you boys." Amanda chuckled as she set the table.

"So really, what's Frank making for you, baby?" Jared asked, and I realized he could sense my change in mood and was trying to distract me. I smiled at him that I understood what he was doing.

"He's making me my favorite." I smiled at him. "Three egg omelet with cheese, bacon, green peppers, onions, tomatoes, and a side of sour cream. It's like heaven in your mouth."

"That does sound really good," Cameron said, turning to Frank. "Can I get one, too, please?"

"Me, too," Jared and Rhyce added together, but Jared continued. "We worked up an appetite coming to someone's aid. We have to talk about that, Tristan."

"Okay, I'm ready," I answered softly with a nod.

"I have a question first," Cameron said, focusing over to Frank, who was cooking up a storm. "Are you drawn to Tristan and his power?"

"I can feel his power, it's growing, and he's not even fully tapped into it," Frank replied with a nod. His eyebrows scrunched together as he went on. "But I'm not drawn to him like I think you mean. I mean he's cute as a button, but he's not my type. No offense, kid."

"None taken." I giggled, before his words sunk in. "That man was lying then, wasn't he?"

"Yeah, I think Ben's full of shit." Cameron nodded as he glanced at Jared. "I've met an Omega before, and I was more than able to control myself. I mean yeah, I felt the pull of his power, but I didn't attack the guy to try and get it."

"I didn't know people would be drawn to me like that." I sighed as I set down my now empty mug. I nuzzled my face in Jared's neck for comfort as his strong arms wrapped around me. "My parents never told me anything about not being able to go out alone. I mean, I've been alone around my pack before without any problems."

"That was when you were still a virgin, baby," Rhyce said calmly as he rubbed my back. "When we had the ceremony, it was like lighting a flame inside of you for your power to grow. That's how it will help us by being with you."

"So that made me grow taller?" I asked, turning my head to look at him with the confusion I felt. "Are you guys feeling any stronger?"

"Yeah, we got to you much faster than I normally would have been able to," Cameron admitted. Then he explained what I'd missed and how they'd found me. It seems my men came back home right after I'd left, and Amanda had told them where I was. They of course realized I could be in danger and immediately drove over to the pack lands.

When they saw Ben's truck there, they hopped out, shifted, and gave chase to where they heard the howls coming from. Then of course, they rescued me, and then we'd all had mind-blowing sex. They realized I was bigger than two days ago, or even yesterday, so they booked it back to the vehicles with a passed out Omega. We got home maybe ten minutes before I woke up on the kitchen table being measured.

"Okay, so break it down for me," I said as I rubbed my temples, trying to relieve the pressure building there. "I can't ever go out alone again because we don't know how pack members *might* react to the power they feel from me or they might be assholes and just try to take it. Fan-fucking-tastic."

"There's a reason the High Council passed the laws about how Omegas need to be treated," Jared whispered as his eyes filled with sympathy. "I know you hate how you were contracted out, but it's for more than just to give the inner circle strength, baby. It's also that every Omega will be protected. Once you hit twenty-one, you're like an untapped atom bomb of power, and some people would do anything to have you."

"That's also why the contracts are with more than just the Alpha," Cameron said as he wiped his hands over his face in frustration. "If the inner circle is strong, it leads to a stable and prosperous pack. But it also makes you have three very strong protectors against anyone who'd want to take you and use you."

"Ben's truck was parked by Rhyce's SUV, right?" I asked, a thought coming to me. All three of them nodded as Frank and Amanda brought over breakfast and then sat down. They weren't eating, but this conversation affected them, too, in a way if I was living there. I mean, Amanda hadn't known I couldn't go off alone either. "Ben had said that Jared wasn't there to protect me. I don't think they just stumbled on me going for a run on the pack grounds guys."

"I agree," Rhyce sighed as he leaned back in his chair. "We have this same meeting every Friday morning with the pack elders. They might have seen my SUV there, but they knew I wasn't in it. It would have been too easy for them to watch the house on the chance you went off alone when they knew we'd be detained. I mean, why were five men not at work on a Friday morning?"

"This just keeps getting better and fucking better," I grumbled as I dug into my breakfast. "And I also want to know why the fuck I'm getting bigger, and how much bigger I might get. None of my clothes are going to fit me. I've already grown three inches in two days for god sakes! I'm so not paying for a new wardrobe."

"We'll figure this out, baby," Jared said as he kissed my neck. I'd turned around on his lap, but he'd kept me there when I went to take a chair of my own. It felt right just to sit and eat on his lap and right then I needed the comfort. "You're not alone in this, Tristan. We're here for you, and we'll get answers."

"I know, I'm just sulking, but I think that's understandable after all of this," I replied. No one said anything either way, but glancing around the table, I saw all the sympathetic stares. It just seemed any time things got a little better in my life, tons more shit was dumped on me. At some point and time it would be more than one person could handle. And while I was glad my men were willing to help bear the load, how much more was coming?

# Chapter 6

"My men need some major fun tonight," I said to Amanda as I walked into the kitchen later that afternoon. Jared, Cameron, and Rhyce had gone to one of the elders' houses and called an emergency meeting to discuss what was going on. They also were going through the pack archives to see if there was anything about Omegas growing randomly.

"I agree," she replied as she glanced over at me.

"It's going to be okay, Amanda. I'm not going anywhere," I said gently before I'd even realized it had come out of my mouth. Hers just about hit the floor as her eyes got wide. I felt myself have a similar reaction as I realized I'd felt her emotions. "Shit, this is new."

"It seems we've found one of your gifts." She nodded.

"It kinda happened with Jared earlier today, but I figured it was because we're, um... ya know, intimate." I shrugged, unable to meet her eyes. "I didn't realize I was barging in on your thoughts or whatever. It was almost as if I heard you say it aloud."

"What did you feel or hear?" Amanda asked, tilting her head as she looked confused.

"That you're worried someone or some ones from the pack will hurt me or take me away from Jared, Cameron, and Rhyce," I answered sheepishly. I felt really bad as if I'd eavesdropped on a private conversation. But it really wasn't my fault I could feel what she was feeling. "You're scared that your boys are happier than you've ever seen them, and if they lost me, it could destroy them and the pack."

"Y-yes t-that's exactly what I-I was thinking," she stuttered out as her eyelashes fluttered. I raced to her, afraid she was going to pass out, but she gripped the counter and started breathing deeply. I rubbed her back gently as we just stood there for a few minutes and seemed to collect ourselves. "This is going to take some getting used to."

"Yeah, that's one way to say it." I snickered as I started to panic. Instantly Amanda wrapped me in her arms, and I felt her confidence that me having this power was a good thing. "I just wish I could kind of have one thing at a time, you know? I mean could everything just stop dumping on me all at once?"

"Not the way life works," she snorted as she patted me on the back again before letting me go. "Now, back to you boys having fun tonight?"

"Well, it seems they all have had feelings for each other, though they're now just admitting." I shrugged, trying to formulate what I was thinking without giving away too much information to the poor woman. "I'm thinking I need to light a firecracker under their asses so to speak."

"I seduced my mate with strip poker." Amanda winked at me. "Worked like a charm."

"Yeah, but if we get naked they all tend to attack me." I blushed as I found my feet very interesting. "I need them to make out with each other."

"Hmm, that is a difficult one," she replied, rubbing her chin in thought.

"What if we didn't bet clothes, but favors instead?" I waggled my eyebrows so she knew what type of *favors* I was implying.

"Oh, you're good." She giggled, and we went into plotting mode.

Amanda and Frank helped me get a bunch of munchies together along with more sandwiches than we could ever eat. Then we got a cooler together of beer, brought a blender up to Jared's suite with all the fixings for margaritas. By the time I'd found a couple of decks of playing cards, it was dinnertime, and I expected them any moment.

"So we went to the kitchen for dinner and were informed it was being held in my room," Jared said with a raised eyebrow as they entered his room. He glanced around the room and took in everything set up. "Poker night?"

"Yup, we need some fun with everything crazy going on," I answered as I finished combing my hair. I'd taken a shower, figuring I'd want to be nice and clean before the festivities began.

"Strip poker then?" Cameron asked as he came around the table I'd set up and gave me a quick kiss before taking a chair.

"Nope." I giggled as they all grabbed beers and food off the platter. I already had a large margarita in front of me as well. "We're going to play for IOUs. I have slips of paper and pens for everyone to write things down on. You have to announce what you're betting though, and if someone doesn't agree to that bet when we're playing, they have to fold."

"Inventive." Rhyce snickered as he licked some mayo off his lips and then leaned over to give me a kiss as well. "Let's get this show on the road. I'm curious to see what I'm going to win."

"Five card stud?" I asked as I started shuffling. Everyone was in agreement as I dealt. They waited for me to make the first bet even though I was the dealer. I studied my hand and realized I already had two pair and was willing to bet big. Reaching for one of the slips of paper and pen, I wrote down my bet as I announced it. "One blow job."

"Seriously?" Jared choked out as beer shot out for his mouth. We all laughed as he mopped himself up, but I did notice Cameron and Rhyce shifting in their seats as the room started to smell of desire. "Okay, I'm in."

"I fold." Rhyce snickered as Cameron agreed to stay in. We each discarded, and I got probably the best card I could have, another ace. That gave me a full house, aces over queens.

"I raise my blow job with one hour in handcuffs," I announced as I wrote it down and threw my slip in the pile.

"Fuck me," Jared groaned as Cameron stared at me with lust in his eyes.

"Just to be clear, what happens during that hour?" Cameron asked as his hand disappeared under the table.

"Whatever the winner wants," I answered, batting my eyelashes before letting my voice get deeper with desire. "And I do mean whatever they want for an entire hour as I'm handcuffed down to their bed, helpless to stop them."

"I'm in," Cameron said as he wrote it down as he swallowed loudly. It turned out Jared folded, which automatically gave the winner a blow job from him. Cameron smiled widely at me, and I saw his canines had extended, meaning he was incredibly turned on. "Whatcha got, baby?"

"Full house, aces over queens." I smirked knowing it was an awesome hand.

"Son of a—," Cameron grumbled as he tossed his cards down on the table. "Do you have handcuffs? Are we doing it now?"

"I can get some." I giggled as I piled up my winning slips and winked at him. "And it's up to the winner as to when, within reason of course."

"My deal." Rhyce snickered as he reached for the cards with one hand and patted Cameron on the back with the other. "I'd love to be a fly on the wall when he's handcuffed to your bed, baby."

"I might have you join in," I purred as I ran my hands down my chest, plucking my nipples through my white cotton shirt. "I get to do whatever I want to him for an hour. Maybe I'll want you and Jared to fuck him."

"Oh sweet hell." Jared gasped as he glanced at Cameron and back to me. "This is the best poker game ever."

"Yeah, we'll see if you feel that way at the end of the night," Cameron growled playfully as he narrowed his eyes at Jared. "You did just lose a blow job."

"I'd blow our baby any time he wants anyways." Jared shrugged as we took our cards as Rhyce dealt. I was just about to finish my first drink and decided to switch to water since I'd learned I was a lightweight. It wouldn't be much fun if I got drunk and the game ended.

"I bet a back rub with happy ending," Rhyce said, smiling like the cat that ate the canary as he wrote it down. We were all in for that one as we discarded and got more.

"I raise with a rim job," Cameron announced as he leered at me. "Tongue, lots and lots of tongue fucking to be exact."

"I'm in," I panted, remembering how his tongue felt on my hole. I swear it was quivering as I squirmed in my chair as I wrote it down on my slip. "I've got three fives."

"Ha!" Jared exclaimed as he laid his cards down. "My flush beats that, baby."

"Fuck, you guys suck," Cameron grumbled as he threw his cards down. "I had two high pair for crying out loud."

"Well, my four of a kind wins," Rhyce growled as he held up his cards. His gaze landed on Jared as he dropped his cards. "I'll take my rimming from you now, please."

"Right now?" Jared asked, his eyes going wide as he glanced from Rhyce to me. "Is that the rules?"

"He can collect now or later, up to him." I shrugged and winked at Rhyce. I should have known he'd totally get what I was up to with my poker night.

"You want your blow job now, baby?" Cameron asked as he pulled off his shirt. "I think it's going to get very hot in here."

"No, I think I'm going to just watch the show," I answered as I unzipped my fly. I yanked off my shirt as well when Jared stood slowly and walked around the table to Rhyce.

"Are you really okay with this?" Rhyce asked Jared softly as he stopped our Alpha's hands at the button of his jeans.

"Fuck yeah," Jared moaned and pulled Rhyce closer, mashing their mouths together. I instantly got hard as I watched their tongues duel for dominance as they started pulling clothes off. I'd have to remember to give myself a pat on the back later for this idea.

Once they were naked, Jared spun Rhyce around and pushed him down on the table. Jared moaned as he knelt behind his Beta and pulled the cheeks of his ass apart.

"I've wanted to touch you like this for so long," Jared whispered as he leaned in and licked Rhyce's hole.

"You could have," Rhyce panted as he fisted his hands on the table. "I hate that we were all idiots and didn't ever admit what we wanted."

"Well, we know now," Cameron said firmly as he met my eyes. "All we needed was our baby to bring us all together. And I know I'll always be grateful to Tristan for that."

"It wasn't like I was trying to be noble." I snorted as I started stroking myself as I watched Jared intently. "I wanted all of us in one bed so I didn't have to bed hop and worry if I was hurting anyone. I never dreamed you all would want me for real much less each other."

"And that's why we're all falling for you," Rhyce whispered and then gasped as Jared pushed his tongue in. "You're the glue that binds us all together, and you truly care about us already after only a few days."

"Kinda hard not to when you three are the men of my dreams," I admitted. I was already so close to coming as I watched Jared enthusiastically eating Rhyce's ass. "Fuck, this is hot."

"Can I touch, too?" Jared asked before diving back in.

"Yes! God, yes, Jared, do whatever you want," Rhyce begged as he spread his legs wider. Rhyce had been sitting to my right as Cameron sat on my left, so he was leaning over me to get a good look.

"Fuck yeah," Cameron groaned as Jared started stroking Rhyce in time with his thrusting tongue. I was so busy watching I didn't even see Cameron move to lean over me further. "I'll still owe you another blow job, but this is just too much to resist."

"What are—" I turned to asked, but was interrupted when he swallowed my cock all the way down. I groaned loudly as I thrust up into his wet heat. It took seconds for me to come after being majorly primed already. I cried out his name as I pumped my dick down his throat, shooting my seed as he swallowed every drop of it.

"You taste like kettle corn." Cameron purred as he licked me clean. I glanced down at his hand and saw he'd come as well. Grabbing his hand, I brought it to my mouth and started licking his cum up. "Shit, baby, I'm going to end up fucking you on the table next to Rhyce."

Just then, Rhyce cried out and shot his load all over Jared's hand as our Alpha was still moaning and tongue fucking his ass. Jared moved to sit in the chair and pulled Rhyce on his lap. They touched, kissed, and cuddled lovingly, and I felt my heart soar that I'd had a part in bringing them together.

"You did that, baby," Cameron whispered in my ear as if hearing my thoughts. And then I felt his hurt that they didn't seem to want him, but he was still glad at least I did.

"They'll prove you wrong before the night is over," I said gently to him as I cupped his cheek in my hand. "You don't see yourself the way the rest of us do, Cameron."

"Shit, you really can feel what we're feeling," he replied, his eyes going wide.

"Not just you guys, but it's not always," I admitted as I pushed my spent dick back in my jeans and zipped them up. They had been a gift that was too big on me always, but now they fit. It was still very disconcerting that I was having some type of growth spurt at twenty-one.

"What's going on now?" Rhyce asked as he stood up with Jared and got dressed. "You're sensing Cameron's emotions?"

"It happened with Jared this morning and Amanda this afternoon," I answered, shooting a glance at Cameron. I could see and feel his panic that I'd tell them what he was feeling. Giving my head a subtle shake, I looked back at Rhyce again so as to not draw attention. I felt him instantly calm down again before I stopped reading anything on him. "I'm not sure how it works. It seems it's really strong emotions. Like Amanda was scared this afternoon."

"What was she afraid of?" Jared asked as he paused and dropped his shirt again, seeming to have decided to leave it off just in case more fun came.

"I-is it fair for me to tell you?" I replied slowly, feeling as if I'd be betraying her confidence. "I mean it's not like she told me herself, you know?"

"That's a good point," Rhyce nodded as he took his seat again, glancing at Jared. "Something we're going to have to discuss as a family. While I get that Tristan won't want to betray people, I can't think he'd be gifted with this if he was supposed to always keep it to himself. Maybe there's a guideline we can think up on when he needs to share with us for the safety of us and the pack?"

"How about we table it until we know for sure what the gift is?" Cameron suggest as he reached over and rubbed my back. "Let's give Tristan a chance to figure it out and adjust for now. Then we can discuss what's fair."

"I agree, unless it's something you feel we should know, baby," Jared said after a few moments. "You're smart, so you'll know if you feel something that could lead to danger or we need to know as the leadership of the pack."

"Thank you," I whispered, my eyes filling with tears as I was touched by their faith in me. Not only that, but worrying about how this would affect me and opting to discuss it between our *family*.

"No, thank you, baby," Rhyce said with a smile as he took my hand. "This is new and confusing I'm sure, but you're open and sharing it with us. That's a huge show of trust in us."

"So, whose turn is it to deal?" Jared asked after a minute or so with no response from me. I just wasn't sure as to what to say. I smiled and squeezed Rhyce's hand as Cameron said it was Jared's turn. The cards were shuffled and dealt again, while Rhyce had made me another drink as we all chatted and stuffed our faces.

Cameron sucked at poker. That was one thing I learned over the next few hands. He'd lost every round and never just folded right away. Part of me wondered if he wanted to have Rhyce and Jared with a pile of favors from him.

I, on the other hand, was cleaning up nicely only having lost one out of the five more hands we played. The round I lost, Jared won a fast, kinky fuck from me in any position he wanted and a shopping date. I thought that one was weird given how dirty we were all being, but then I realized it wasn't about just getting off. We were all betting things that gave and brought pleasure. That and worked on getting to know each other better.

"I see on the bet for a home cooked picnic," I said, smiling at Cameron's bet. He'd stipulated that neither Amanda nor Frank could help with the preparations to for the picnic. "And I raise love slave for a week, including costume of thong and chains."

"I-I'm sorry, come again?" Rhyce sputtered as everyone stared at me like I'd lost it.

"What? Is a week too long?" I asked with a smirk, knowing full well I was bluffing since I had shit in my hand.

"No, I'll take that bet," Jared answered with lust in his eyes. I shivered without even meaning to as I had all type of images in my head as to what he'd do to me over that week. I figured they'd all fold and I'd win the picnic, getting a chance to have one with each of them individually. He turned and looked at Rhyce and then Cameron. "You guys going to chicken out?"

"Fuck, I've already lost every hand." Cameron chuckled as he picked up his cards. "Fine, I'm in."

"I'll have our baby for a love slave for a week, because I think he's bluffing." Rhyce smirked, and I wanted to groan at how my plan backfired. Reaching for the three cards, I couldn't even help laughing at what I saw. I was totally going to win. I'd had the ten and queen of hearts and now just got the jack, king, and ace.

"You guys are so fucked," I said as I held my cards to my chest. "Anyone want to raise me before we show what we've got?"

"Yes, I raise a month of additional overnights as love slave," Jared answered, and it hit me like a ton of bricks what he was feeling.

He was sad. He thought Cameron and Rhyce were wanting to be with him so they'd be able to be my mate. Jared felt that if they'd really wanted him, they would have said something years ago. He was thinking that he was the reason I was here, but the three of us would gladly be a family without him.

I tilted my head to study him without even meaning to, and I saw his eyes go wide. "Tristan, that's not exactly fair, baby."

"Huh, what?" I asked as if snapping out of a trance. "You raise a month. I got it."

"You also got everything I was thinking and feeling, didn't you?"

"Shit, I'm sorry, I didn't mean to," I answered as I put my cards face down and pulled my knees up to my chest in the chair. "It's hard to explain it. The only way I can almost think it compares to is a really good orgasm."

"One more time?" Rhyce asked, raising an eyebrow.

"You know how when you come really hard and you see those lights behind your eyes and you're there but not all there because you're so focused on the person who'd just made you come like that?" I rambled trying to get my point across.

"Yeah, like you're kind of still connected to them and you're moving slowly," Cameron said with a nod as his eyebrows scrunched together. "So you orgasm every time you get a reading?"

"No, it's that focus I'm referring to," I answered, shaking my head. "Like for a few moments I'm not really here but inside the other person when I catch a snippet of what they're feeling. Every time it's happened before I even realize what's going on. It's like I look at them and see something and then suddenly everything they're feeling and some of what they're thinking is dumped on me."

"What was I thinking?" Jared asked, looking partially pissed and daring me at the same time.

"Don't do this, Jared," I whispered as tears filled my eyes. "This isn't my fault, okay? I wouldn't turn around and tell everyone what I felt from you. Don't make me feel bad about this when I can't control it."

The last words were barely out of my mouth before I was lifted up and into his arms. "I'm so sorry, baby. I'm such an asshole."

"No you're not," I said firmly as I wrapped myself around him. "I get why you'd be pissed, but I can't control this, Jared."

"I know you can't," he replied as he held me tight and sat down in my chair. "I was just thinking and feeling something very private, and for you to have known it pissed me off. It felt like you were reading my journal or something, and I lashed out. But you're right, and you're not doing it on purpose, being nosey, or trying to betray me. It's not fair to get mad at you."

"Thank you for understanding." I sighed before lowering my voice so only he would hear as I whispered in his ear. "Don't feel that way, my big Alpha. Cameron thinks you guys don't want him and Rhyce was the one who said first that he wanted us to all be a family but didn't know how to make it happen until you found me. Not that I'm sure what that means, but he said I had to ask you."

"I promise to explain it when I know you're ready to hear it," Jared said softly as he kissed my neck. "Thank you for telling me all of that. You really are more than able to know when to tell what you learn or keep it to yourself. I know you'd never gossip or start shit, but you'll help when you can."

"So…Who won?" Cameron asked, breaking the trance we were in.

"I did," we both answered, and I knew neither of us was talking about poker.

"Well according to the cards, Tristan did," Rhyce snickered as Jared and I turned back towards the table. He gave me a soft kiss before going back to his seat and leaving me in mine. Rhyce gave me a scathing looking. "You were totally bluffing until you got more cards, weren't you?"

"Oh hells yeah." I giggled as I gestured to the pile of betting slips. "Did every one stay in for Jared's raise?"

"Yes," Cameron playfully groaned with a smile. "You won the mother lode, baby. Each of us your personal love slave for a full week and four more weeks of nights, plus personal picnic with us. So, you thought of this fun evening because you're a card shark, huh?"

"Promise you won't get mad?" I asked, glancing around at all of them as I made sure to scoot back my chair a bit, feet on the floor. I had a feeling I'd need to run after I admitted the answer to his question. I waited until each of them nodded or grunted their concession. "I had to look up how to play poker. That's why I said five card stud. It's the most basic of the games. This was my first time playing, ever."

"Why you little—," Jared shouted as he lunged for me over the table. I was up and out of my chair in a flash.

"Fucking beginners luck," Rhyce grumbled as he tried to catch me. I made it to the door, but didn't get it open in time before I was lifted off my feet. Letting out a very un-grown-up yelp as I was thrown over Rhyce's massive shoulder, I tried to wiggle free. "We might owe you everything in that stack of betting slips, but you set up tonight for us to have fun."

"And fun with you we shall have," Jared purred as he tore my jeans off of me.

"Jared, those were the only jeans I had left that fit," I whined. But I couldn't help the smile that followed at their antics and obvious desire for me.

"We'll get you more," Rhyce said as he smacked my naked ass. "Cameron, go grab the box under my bed. We need handcuffs and lots of toys to drive our baby wild."

"Oh fuck me," I groaned as I went hard against his shoulder.

"We will, all night long," Jared growled as I was tossed on the bed. Looking up at the three smiling faces, I spread my arms out wide in an invitation. I knew I wouldn't even pretend to deny it anymore that I was all theirs in every way possible. They wanted me for more than my being an Omega and a toy. And that's all I ever wanted in life.

# Chapter 7

I woke up the next morning sprawled over my men in Jared's bed. They'd been good to their word and fucked me all night long. I swear I lost count on how many orgasms I had, much less how many they'd had. Groaning softly as I climbed out of bed, I fell to the floor when my legs wouldn't work.

What the fuck was up with that?

I moved my hands out in front of me in time to catch my fall, trying not to laugh when I saw that I still had handcuffs locked around my right wrist. It was quite enlightening to find out how much fun they could be. I'd never have guessed Rhyce was into kinky sex like that. But the toy box he had said otherwise. And I loved every second of the handcuffs, vibrators, dildos, and various other toys they'd used on me.

Pushing back up, I wobbled my way to the bathroom. I couldn't believe I was this sore from our sex marathon. I mean, I could see being tender, maybe some muscle cramping, but I swear my bones hurt. When I leaned over the counter to turn on the water so I could wash up, I got a glimpse as to why I might be in pain.

"Help me! Someone get in here," I screamed at the top of my lungs, completely panicking. "Guys, something's very wrong."

"What is it, baby?" Jared asked as I heard him race towards me. He gasped, and I met his eyes in the mirror as I saw the same fear written on his face that I felt. "Tristan?"

"Yeah, it's me," I answered, even my voice sounded deeper. "What's happening to me, Jared? I'm actually in pain today."

"You better eat right now," Rhyce said, coming into the bathroom as he wrapped an arm around my waist for support. "Jesus, you're almost as tall as I am now."

"And still a twig," I cried out, more in pain as we walked back into the bedroom than distress. Though I had a feeling that was coming as well. "How can someone grow seven inches over night?"

"Can it be an inch for every time we have sex with you?" Cameron asked, his eyes going wide, and I felt his panic as much as my own.

"Stop it," I yelled at him as Rhyce sat me on the bed. "Stop it right now. You cannot panic okay? I'm fucking freaked out enough as is, and if you guys start freaking, I'll feel it and freak even more."

"Okay, it's okay, baby," Rhyce cooed as he pointed to Cameron. "Get the robe from Jared's closet for Tristan. We need to get him something to eat and drink. He's going to need extra fuel after all of this, and I'm worried about him passing out."

"Right," Cameron said, getting into action. I met Jared's eyes, and saw more than I ever wanted to know and feel from him. He quickly glanced away as he changed what he was thinking about, but it was too late.

"You bastard," I gasped as the tears started to fall. I pushed away from Rhyce, stood, took the few steps to Jared, and slapped him hard across the face. "You're doing this to me, and *you're* upset about it? I fucking grew over half a foot last night and I'm in pain, and you're making this all about you? Fuck you, Jared."

"Tristan, wait, I'm sorry, okay?" He begged, reaching for me. "I can't help the thoughts in my head, okay? It doesn't mean I don't want you anymore, baby—"

"Fuck you, don't call me that ever again," I spat out as I grabbed the robe from Cameron. I felt confusion, fear, and sorrow coming from Rhyce and Cameron. And that sorrow was what got me. They felt the same as Jared did. I stared daggers at both of them as I yanked the robe on and headed towards the door. "And you're both just as bad. Fuck all of you. I thought you cared about me, really could love me. But if this is how you feel about this, then none of you did."

"What did we do?" Cameron asked, and I felt more confusion coming off of him. But I'd had enough. I didn't answer as I stumbled out the door. I heard them talking as I made my way to the stairs leaning on the walls heavily. "What did he feel from us that he's so pissed?"

"I was feeling sad and thinking I would miss him being able to sit on my lap and that he used to fit perfectly in my arms," Jared cried, and him saying it aloud hurt just as bad as when I felt it. "It just came into my head. It doesn't mean I don't care about him just the same. But I liked him being our pint-size baby that I could carry around and have his hot little body wrapped around me, you know?"

"Yeah, I was thinking the same thing," Rhyce admitted as I reached the top of the stairs.

I couldn't hear anymore, my heart was already shattered, and now it was like a knife in my back. This was happening to me because of them, from having sex with them and making them stronger. And they were thinking about how this would affect *them*? Fuck them, I was gone as soon as I was able to sneak away. I wouldn't live like this.

We didn't know why I was growing, if I would ever stop, or how it was even happening. All I knew is it happened after sex with them. So if they were going to be selfish and pout because I wouldn't fit on their goddamn laps anymore instead of worrying about me and hell, maybe feeling guilty for doing this to me. I was gone. It was over.

Amanda gasped as I stumbled into the kitchen. She and Frank helped me to a chair and immediately started to bustle about. Next thing I knew there was muffins, juice, milk, and coffee in front of me as she was talking to me.

"I'm sorry, what?" I asked trying to snap out of my daze. I'd been so hungry and thirsty when I'd gotten up, but now... now I just felt cold and wanted to crawl in a deep, dark black hole.

"Where are the boys? Why are you stumbling in here alone?" She said, panic in her voice and flowing off of her in waves. "How is this happening?"

"I don't know, Amanda," I whispered as the tears started to fall again. "And I'm alone because they're assholes who were so fucking focused on how this affected *them* that I told them where they could stick it. I'm over a half a foot taller than I was yesterday, and they're upset about how I look and fit with them physically."

"They didn't say that," she denied as she sat down next to me, glancing at Frank who shrugged.

"No, I felt it," I said, meeting her glance, and I saw the tears forming in her eyes as she understood what I was getting at. "I felt their sorrow that I wouldn't be little anymore and fit in their arms. That I didn't look like me anymore a-and t-that I wasn't their Tristan anymore."

"And that's why we're assholes," Rhyce whispered as they approached the table.

"I've never once raised my voice or yelled at you boys," Amanda said in a tone so cold I even shivered as she stood up and faced them. "I've loved you as if you were sons of my own and have always been proud of you, until today. You should be ashamed of yourselves! You don't even deserve Tristan. *You did this to him,* and you don't even feel guilty about it?"

"We're sorry—" Cameron started to say, but Amanda cut him off, yelling at the top of her lungs.

"Too little too late, Cameron! You need to leave him be while we try to tend to him and figure out what's going on. You'd think the men who supposedly care for him would have done that, but no, they're selfish pricks."

"Amanda," Jared growled but didn't get any further when Frank grabbed the Alpha's arm.

"Go now before I call the elders and find Tristan sanctuary from you," Frank said firmly, and I realized it was the first time I'd seen him not smiling. "This is borderline neglect of a mate, and he doesn't want you around. You need to respect that and grovel later if he'll let you."

"Tristan, baby? Please, let us help you," Rhyce begged, but didn't come any closer to me.

"Fuck you, Rhyce, I'm not your baby since I don't fit in your arms," I replied, closing my eyes so I didn't have to look at them. The tears kept falling as the pain in my body continued. "I hurt. I'm in physical pain, okay? Just leave me the fuck alone unless you have answers as to what's going on or how to help me.

"I trusted you to figure this out before it got worse, but you didn't. Instead, I gave myself to you three, heart, body, and soul. And the first issue that's not my fault, none of you were there for me. Instead, you're wrapped in your own selfish feelings about my looks and size. That's not being a mate or caring about the man you're fucking. You got power from me, you got what you paid for, now leave me be so I can heal."

"Get out," Amanda snarled after a few minutes of them just standing there staring at me. I could feel all of their emotions, and none of it helped. Oh sure, they felt guilty as all hell now, but that didn't mean shit to me. It was too late. Whatever love had been growing for them inside of me was gone, replaced with hate and sorrow.

"We're sorry, Tristan," Cameron whispered as they left.

"Okay, time to get some fuel in you," Amanda said firmly as she sat back down next to me. I shook my head as the tears poured out of my eyes.

"What's the point? I don't care anymore, and it's not like I'll be growing anymore since they don't even want to touch me," I sobbed as I buried my head in my arms.

"Tristan, do you trust me?" she whispered as she ran her fingers through my hair. I nodded as I continued to cry. "Then you need to fuel up, okay? Normal growth spurts can screw with someone's hormones and emotions, sweetheart. I know you've been hurt, but it might be fixable with time. Let's not give up all hope just yet. Trust me to help you now, please, Tristan?"

"Okay," I answered after a few moments and sat back up, wiping my eyes with the heels of my now large hands. "If you promise to keep them away from me, I won't fight you and do what you want. Deal?"

"For now." She nodded and then sighed as she stood up to get me more food. I ate like a garbage disposal, not even sure where the hell I put it all. Frank cooked nonstop as I inhaled at least a dozen pancakes, several muffins, and enough bacon and sausage to make up a large pig. Amanda only let me have one mug of coffee, which I couldn't even drink considering it came from the present they'd given me.

Instead, I drank glass after glass of milk and orange juice. Amanda gave me several ibuprofen, assuring me the dose was okay since she called the pack doctor. She informed me he would be by later after talking with the elders and coming up with a plan on how to help me.

When I was done eating, Amanda grabbed several sports drinks as Frank helped me back upstairs. He stayed in the bathroom while I showered in case I needed him, being completely discreet and very fatherly. The pain was immeasurable. It seemed now that the fear and adrenaline wore off, I was feeling everything

Frank helped me into bed, and the doctor showed up right after I was all tucked in. He set a workout schedule to help my new larger muscles and joints along with a regiment of muscle relaxers and topographic cream. Doc Holiday, yes, I laughed at the name, had put a call into a friend of his on the High Council and hoped we'd get answers soon.

Everyone left me after Amanda made me take my pills and drink another bottle of Gatorade. It was maybe a half an hour later when I heard a timid knock at the door. I was already mostly asleep and tried to ignore it.

"Leave now," I growled as Cameron walked into my room and closed the door behind me. "You heard Amanda and Frank."

"Amanda said I could come after I talked to her," he said softly as he walked over and sat down on my bed. "Just answer me one question, and if after that you really want me to go, I'll leave and not bother you again."

"Fine," I ground out.

"What was I feeling this morning in Jared's room?"

"What?" I asked, turning to look at him finally as my anger and confusion battled.

"What was I feeling this morning in Jared's room?" He asked again, moving closer to me. "You said you felt my panic, and I think you got more specific readings off of Jared, but what was I feeling exactly?"

"You were sad, confused, and afraid," I whispered, thinking I understood where he was going with this line of questioning. "But I didn't get anything more than that with everything going on."

"I kept my mouth shut for years how I felt about Rhyce and Jared," Cameron said softly as he moved even closer, lying down next to me. "And it was a bonehead move. I swore I'd never make that mistake again, Tristan. When they told me what they were feeling and why you got so upset, I realized I couldn't keep my mouth shut this time. I can't risk losing you over a misunderstanding."

"What misunderstanding?" I asked, turning towards him. I wanted to yell at the part of my heart that was suddenly filled with hope, but staring into Cameron's eyes, I saw the same fear of rejection I was feeling.

"I was scared, so scared because of what's happening to you," he whispered as he pulled me to him. "I felt afraid that you'd hate us because of what's going on and blame us. I'm scared because the man I'm falling in love with is hurting and I can't stop it or fix it."

"You're falling for me?" I gasped, scooting closer so that our lips were almost touching. "I thought you were all sad because I wasn't small anymore and wouldn't want me."

"Yes, I'm totally falling for you, baby. I was sad because you were in pain and freaking out," he replied before brushing his lips over mine. "It never crossed my mind about how you wouldn't be small anymore. I was sad that you're having to go through this. And I didn't feel guilty until later because we didn't do this on purpose, you have to know that. I mean once I thought about it and realized it was our fault for being with you, yeah, I feel guilty."

"I thought you were being selfish, I'm sorry."

"Don't be sorry, baby," Cameron said as his eyes filled with tears. "This is more than anyone should ever have to go through, and you're allowed to freak out. But I couldn't just sit by and let you think the worst when it's not how I felt. So I talked to Amanda and told her everything. She gave me the green light to come and try and talk to you."

"I'm glad she did."

"And this whole idea that I won't want you because you're not a pip-squeak anymore just isn't true," he said firmly as he rolled on top of me. Cameron was incredibly careful and gentle as he ground his erection against my hip. "Does this feel like I don't want you? You're still sexy as all hell, baby. But I'm falling for the kind-hearted, loving, funny, smart man you are, not just the package you come in. Did I like you being small and letting us carry you around? Yes, I liked it a lot."

"But I'm not that size anymore," I cried out, trying to get away from him as he talked about my worst fear.

"So fucking what?" He growled, punctuating each word with a thrust of his hips. "You're more than a twink to me, Tristan. I was scared for you, wanted to help you, and you shut me out. I wanted to pull you into my arms and make it all better and I couldn't, so I was sad and confused. Just because you got that from us doesn't mean you know exactly why we were feeling that way."

"I heard Jared loud and clear," I snarled as I wiped away my tears. "Fine, I shouldn't have jumped to conclusions as to why you and Rhyce were feeling that way, but I *heard* Jared's thoughts."

"Then that's something you have to take up with him," Cameron said as he cupped my cheek. "But you need to know that he's a mess, baby. I get why you'd be pissed at him for his initial reaction, I do. He can't help his thoughts and feelings, Tristan, no more than you can help hearing and feeling them. It's what he does with those feelings that counts, and his immediate reaction was to help you."

"Not soon enough," I replied and tried to pull away. I could forgive Cameron, but I didn't need him to come in here and be an advocate for forgiving Jared.

"No, you are not going to bolt again," he growled as he held me down firmly by my shoulders. He lightened his hold when I winced in pain, but I stopped fighting him. "There are things you need to know about how you ended up here. I've begged Jared to tell you, but he's afraid you'll leave if you know."

"I can't—" I started to argue, but Cameron cut me off.

"We know about the secret accounts and passports, baby," he said firmly with a raised eyebrow, daring me to refute it and lie to him. "We're in charge of the safety of seventy plus pack members, and it's our jobs to know everything there is to know about someone. The only reason I bring this up is because I'm scared you'll leave if he doesn't tell you how he bid for your contract."

"You say he's upset?" I asked, not meaning to sound callous or like I wanted Jared to suffer, but if he was upset he might still want me then.

"Yeah, he's in a ball on his bed, completely destroyed," Cameron nodded. "He won't talk to me or Rhyce, and he just keeps sobbing that he's lost you for good. It sucks that was his initial reaction to your new size, and yeah, I can see wanting to smack him for it. But it wasn't his *only* reaction, Tristan. You need to hear his other ones and give him a chance to show you that he cares instead of just reading his feelings that he can't control."

"Okay, help me to him," I said after a few moments. Cameron was right. I'd flown off the handle and while I think I was allowed given the situation, Jared had earned the right for me to hear him out. I'd not been fair to him or our mating. He deserved a chance to explain.

"See, that's the big heart I love so much," Cameron cooed, giving me a quick kiss before rolling off the bed and reaching for me. I rolled my eyes at his antics as he helped me out of bed. When I stood up, I was only about two inches shorter than Cameron. He glanced at me as if able to read my thoughts. "Yeah, it's going to take some getting used to. But you're still the man we want, just not so compact."

"I hope so," I whispered as he wrapped an arm around my waist. I leaned on him heavily since my bones and muscles still felt like gelatin as we left my room and made it across the hall. Rhyce rushed over to us as we entered the room, having been seated on the bed. "Jared first, then you."

"Guess I'm never going to be your priority," Rhyce said as he went to move back. I reached out and grabbed his wrist before he could get far.

"Him first because he's the one I'm furious with," I replied firmly. "I have no doubt in my mind that you and I just need to iron things out like Cameron and I just did. But Jared's suffering. Would you rather I just leave him like that while we kiss and make up?"

"No, but I thought you were just as pissed at me," he said as he shook his head. "So it's not that you care about Jared more than me?"

"No, I love all of you idiots equally," I replied, pulling him in for a kiss. "And you'll always be my special mate who defied his Alpha to make sure I was happy. If anything, I fell for you first, Rhyce."

"I love you, too, baby," Rhyce whispered against my lips and then kissed me. "We'll get you through this, okay?"

"Even if I can't fit on your lap or in your arms anymore?" I asked, tears filling my eyes. I was scared for his answer, but I was also sad that I wouldn't fit anymore. I'd loved when they picked me up, carried me, or pulled me onto their laps. It made me feel so special and loved.

"Fuck that, I'm strong enough to still carry you," Rhyce growled as he swooped me up into his arms to make his point. "And I don't care if you crush my lap, you're still going to sit on it and ride me like a cowboy."

"After we figure out what's going on and get me my hat," I teased as he carried me to the bed. Jared still hadn't moved or stopped crying since we came into the room, and I realized he was in such a deep sorrow, he was about drowning in it. I glanced back at Rhyce, who nodded at me as he laid me down next to Jared, confirming my suspicions. Despair was rolling off Jared in such strong waves I could feel that it made me gasp.

"Don't you have more pills coming soon?" Cameron asked as he gestured to Rhyce that they should leave. "We'll go get them and some lunch for everyone. We need to make sure our baby's fed."

"Yeah, I'm hungry again," I answered rolling my eyes as they left. I turned back to Jared and ran my hand over his shoulder. "Jared? I'm here, Jared, it's Tristan. I'm here to listen and so we can talk."

"Baby?" He gasped and rolled over to face me. Instantly his hands were on my face, as he pulled me down to kiss him. "Please don't leave me, Tristan. I'm so fucking sorry. I know you must hate me, but I didn't mean it, okay?"

"I don't hate you, but I think it's time I get some answers." I sighed against his lips. "Starting with whatever you're keeping from me about how I got contracted to this pack. You've said you'd tell me when I was ready to listen, and it's that time, Jared. So start talking."

Jared searched my eyes for a few moments before nodding. "I've been desperately in love with you since you were seventeen, Tristan."

Well, fuck. That was so not what I was expecting. I just stared at him with my mouth hanging open. I had a slew of questions for him including, how, why, when, and all the other basics. But right then, I couldn't get my mouth to work. Instead, I kissed him again.

# Chapter 8

"After I became Alpha of our pack, I traveled for a few months meeting other Alphas and making introductions," Jared explained, his hands still holding my face tenderly. "I had a meeting with the Alpha of the Chicago pack, and he invited me to a Green Bay Packers game. It was also so he could intro me to the Green Bay Alpha..."

"Who's my father," I whispered as the pieces started to fall into place. "We went to a game for my seventeenth birthday. I got tickets from a friend of mine, and my dad demanded I go with him since he's a crazed fan."

"I saw you that day." He nodded. "We were sitting close to you and during halftime we came over."

"I remember you," I gasped as the memories flooded my brain. I remembered not wanting to look at the visiting Alpha because he was so hot. "We never even talked though."

"No, your father wouldn't let me when I asked," Jared agreed as he stroked my cheek. "I saw this gorgeous teenager who hid from me as his cheeks blushed. Your father was pissed because he could smell both of our desire for each other. When we ran with your pack on the full moon, your dad swore he'd deny my bid for you if I dared talk to you. He was worried that I'd sway you towards me with promises of a real life and mate."

"You told him you wanted me back then?" I asked, my eyes going wide in shock. "But I was so tiny and wimpy."

"You were the most beautiful thing I'd ever seen," he said firmly as lust filled his eyes. "I felt like a creep for wanting you when you were only seventeen, but you didn't look that young. You looked like you do now, just maybe not as skinny. But when we met, I meant it when I said I'd waited years to be with you."

"I thought you meant you'd waited years to fuck an Omega."

"No, Tristan, I fell for you before I even knew you were an Omega," he said, kissing me again. "I went to your dad to ask for his blessing to court you after the game. He told me you were an Omega and would never have a mate. The idea of you ever being touched by someone else made me want to kill your father since he'd pick who you'd go to. I came home and told Rhyce and Cameron. They agreed to help me convince the pack that we needed an Omega."

"Stop, just stop, okay?" I cried, pulling away from him. He was telling me that he experienced love at first sight with me, except I didn't look like that anymore.

"Why? I'm telling you that I loved you and never cared you were an Omega!"

"You fell in love with me at first sight," I whispered as I moved off the bed and promptly fell on my ass when my shaky legs didn't support me. "Look at me, Jared! Do I look anything like that person you loved?"

"Yes, yes you do, baby," he said desperately as he crawled onto the floor with me. "So what that you're taller? I don't care that we're the same height or that you're bigger. I was sad about your growing because I didn't know if you'd still want me if you couldn't sit in my lap. Did I like how you'd cuddle with me and fit in my arms? Yes, but not as much as I love the man you are, Tristan.

"I fell in love with you all over again when you demanded your own room and put me in place the night of the ceremony. You weren't just some submissive Omega that would blindly follow my lead. You stood up for yourself and looked at me as an equal. I love you, Tristan. And if I have to sit in your lap so we can cuddle, I'll gladly do it to be by you. You can carry me around when you're nine feet tall if you want."

"Will I really get that big?" I gasped, fear coursing through my veins.

"Fuck! I always stick my foot in my mouth," Jared swore as he sat back on his feet and rubbed his hands over his face. "I don't know. There have been some reports about mates growing bigger when they feel they need to protect their mates. But nothing like this, and we found documents about small Omegas. So it might just be connected to your power, but we don't know yet."

"You really love me?" I asked after a moment, deciding to focus on one issue at a time.

"Yes, with all my heart," he whispered as tears fell down his cheeks. "I'm sorry for my reaction, but I was scared for so many reasons. Way more than the couple you picked up on, okay? I can't help that's what went through my head or you heard, but it's really not all that I felt."

"Yeah, Cameron helped me see that." I nodded as I reached for him. "I love you, too, Jared."

"So you won't use the passports and fall off the planet?" He asked, burying his face in my neck. "If you really want to run, I'll help you, but I want you to stay, baby. I want my mate. You bit me, remember? I'm your mate now, and you're supposed to keep me."

"I'm keeping you," I whispered in his hair as he sobbed against my shoulder. I'd been pissed about what I'd felt off them and their initial reactions. But I'd not stopped long enough to think about how this all affected my men, too. Jared pulled me into his lap as we wrapped around each other in comfort.

"Glad you made up," Cameron said after clearing his throat. We glanced up and saw Rhyce and Cameron's arms loaded with food and drinks. "Amanda made me promise to report how much you ate. That woman is fiercely protective of you."

"You kid yourselves." I snickered as we stood up, and Jared helped me to the table in his seating area. They all looked at me with confusion, and I rolled my eyes before explaining. "Sure, she likes me and all, but she's so worried about me because if something happens to me she thinks it will crush you three. That, and destroy the pack."

"She's right," Rhyce said as he pulled out my chair and kissed my neck as I sat down. "It would kill us to lose you."

"So let's just make sure that doesn't happen," Cameron replied firmly with a nod. He handed me my pills and sports drink, watching me like a hawk that I swallowed them. I filled them in on everything the doctor said as they kept pushing more food at me.

It seemed no matter my size now, they were determined to baby and pamper me. Cameron announced he would be in charge of my pills and morning workouts. Rhyce took over my afternoon massages and vitamins. Jared would monitor my food and nightly stretching. And we all agreed that no more sex until we got answers as to what was happening to me.

That last part was kind of depressing. I mean, I'd just made up with my men and I had to miss out on my first makeup sex? But then again I was in pain, and sex really wasn't an option anyways. And also, I'd grown ten inches over the past few days, and the idea of growing any more would keep me from being horny.

* * * *

The next couple of weeks were difficult, but my men helped me through it. The workouts helped me get used to my larger body, and I was packing on muscle like there was no tomorrow. I'd also grown some more, so we'd found out that while the sex made all of us stronger in the way an Omega worked, it wasn't necessarily to blame. Also, we'd learned from other Omegas that this wasn't always the case.

So after three weeks I had kind of capped out at six-eight. Three inches taller than my mates Cameron and Rhyce. Even though I hadn't claimed Cameron yet, he'd asked me to take his hand in holy mating. It had made me smile at the way he'd phrased it. For someone who was a nervous rambler and constantly called himself a bonehead, he really was a sweetheart. He even went so far as getting down on one knee when he'd asked me.

Jared ordered a custom-size massive bed, and we all slept in it together every night since we'd all made up. I still had my room, but I mainly used it for storage and as an office when I worked. My workouts were changing from basic cardio and stretching to bulking up and working on building strength.

I was taking my daily five mile run around the grounds when I smelled Ben and his crew. My first instinct was to hide, so I ducked behind some trees and kept a lookout for them. Why were they on the Alpha house's land? It couldn't be to bring us a fruit basket, I was pretty sure.

"Come out, come out wherever you are, Omega," Ben taunted, and I was filled with rage. I saw them all approaching and decided to give them a taste of their own medicine. Leaning against the tree I was by, I crossed my massive arms over my built chest and smirked at them. "Holy shit, you're huge!"

"Awww, poor shit head," I crooned as I rolled my eyes. "Can't come rape the poor small Omega now, can you?"

"There's still five of us," he sneered as his friends darted glances to Ben. I was pretty sure they were ready to tell Ben to fuck off.

"Bring it on fucker," I growled as I adjusted my neck and let it pop.

Ben launched at me first with two others right behind him. I spun as I grabbed Ben around the throat and slammed him into the tree. The second one landed on my back, and I was able to toss him about ten yards or so away into another tree. I laughed as I moved out of the third guy's way quickly, and he punched the tree, cussing up a storm at the pain.

"Why me?" I snarled at Ben when he tried to get up. He stumbled a bit as I slammed my fist into the fourth guy's face so hard it knocked him out.

"This should be my pack," Ben answered as he landed on his ass again. "My family has been here for way longer than Jared's. And if I had you and your power as an Omega, I'd be able to beat him for Alpha."

"Sucks to be you then." I snickered as I threw the fifth guy into Ben. I felt like throwing my hands in the air and doing a dance as if I'd made a perfect strike bowling. Instead, the third guy jumped on my back. I reached back and smacked his head hard before tossing him into the pile.

"Guess we're not needed." Cameron laughed from behind me. I turned and saw the wide smiles on my men's faces as they stared at the damage I'd done.

"I love you for being here though," I replied as I went to give them each a kiss. "Can I do it again sometime? That was wicked fun! I've never been in a fight before."

"We'll see, slugger." Rhyce chuckled as he hugged me to him. "Let's not go looking for fights or starting bar brawls just yet, okay?"

"No, but I've been feeling the need to wrestle with my men," I growled as I cupped his groin aggressively. "I sleep with three fucking hot men and have been living like a priest."

"We agreed no sex," Jared said as he wrapped his arms around me from behind. "We were kind of waiting for you to change that rule."

"Let's handle the trash first," I replied, gesturing to the men I'd whooped. "And then I'm invoking some of my winnings from poker night."

"I'll get my thong ready for you, baby." Cameron snickered as he gave me a quick kiss.

That got a laugh from all of us as we started dragging Ben's men back to the house. Three of the five were unconscious, and the other two were howling in pain.

"Ben thinks he should have been Alpha because his family's been part of the pack longer," I said to Jared after we tied them all up in the garage. "They thought if they had me, they'd be strong enough to take you guys on. I seemed to have shocked them with my new size. Guess you didn't tell the pack that your Omega grew over a foot, huh?"

"Didn't want to tell anyone but the elders until we knew why." Jared shrugged as we headed into the kitchen. "I need to call the High Council and inform them that they're getting prisoner transport. Ben and his guys won't be a problem any longer."

"You're upset they'll be put to death," I whispered as I pulled him into my arms. I felt the pain and guilt coming off of him that this was the outcome. "They broke pack laws, Jared. I get why you're upset, but I'd rather it be them than you ending up with a bullet in your head or something. They're not good guys who play fair."

"I know, but it still hurts," he said as he nuzzled his face in my chest. It still was a trip for me that I was five inches taller than my big bad Alpha and he barely reached my shoulders. "I can't help but wonder if I was a better Alpha that maybe they would have been on our side, you know?"

"I do, but I think they were power hungry douches," I answered, kissing the top of his head before leaning down to lick his lips. "I also think we might have the answer as to why I've grown like a weed."

"What do you mean?" Jared asked, confusion in his eyes as he licked my mouth back.

"You found research that mates can grow like crazy when they feel their mates are in trouble," I whispered as I ran my hands down his back in a comforting gesture. "You had a major threat against you, my mate. Somehow, some way my body realized it and that you were my mate before I'd even bit you, Jared. Omega power or not, this was about protecting my mate and the man I love."

"I love you, too, Tristan."

"And I love you both, three," Cameron said as he wrapped his arms around both of us. "I love these group hugs. They make me feel warm and fuzzy inside. And hard. I thought I should mention that they get me hard, too."

"Goofball." Rhyce snickered as he joined in the hug. "We've been the big men on campus or in the pack if you will, all of our lives. Now we have this amazing mate who's our protector. I don't know about you two knuckleheads, but I've never felt so safe and loved in all my life."

"Plus, Tristan's just fucking hot," Cameron purred as he gave me a wink. "But yeah, it's nice to feel that someone will keep me safe for a change instead of the other way around."

"Guess we have more than one reason you've become massive." Jared snickered, and I raised an eyebrow at him in question. "You gave us what we all needed, baby, what we'd always wanted. You're our protector. You're the one who makes us a family and keeps us together while taking care of all of us."

"You're the one who keeps us secure," Rhyce said as he ran his hands over my chest. "And I'm not just talking about our safety. You keep us secure in our relationship and our leadership. You're a big, badass Omega with the power and strength to beat up five adult werewolves without breaking a sweat."

"I like that." I smiled widely. "Big, badass Omega. I should get that in a T-shirt. Maybe Omega would stop being associated with weak or wimpy if more people saw me."

"As long as it's not naked," Jared said with a wink as he pulled away from us. "Because I swear your cock grew as many inches as you did."

"Yeah well, get ready, love slave," I growled as I smacked his butt. "Because I'm going to pound it into your ass all night long as soon as this is handled."

"Oh fuck, I've always wanted to bottom," he groaned as he quickened his pace to his office. I shared a look with Cameron and Rhyce, who seemed just as shocked as I did. Alpha Jared was just full of surprises it seemed. I couldn't help but wonder what else he had in store for us and if he'd like being a bottom.

# Chapter 9

"I cannot believe you're making me wear this," Jared grumbled from his bathroom.

"I could just fuck you in front of the entire pack for your first time if you prefer," I said as sweetly as I could. The reply growl I got told me exactly how much Jared liked that idea. "A bet is a bet, unless you want to go back on it."

"I keep my word," he replied as he stepped out into the bedroom. I just about swallowed my tongue at the sight of him. He might have bitched about the tiny thong I'd picked out for each of them for when they'd be my love slave, but damn he looked fantastic. I let my gaze roam over every inch of his firm, muscled body. He seemed to glisten, showing off his definition.

"Oil?" I croaked out after a couple of tries.

"I figured if I was going to be your love slave, I should make sure my body was ready for your wicked ways," Jared said in a sultry voice as he sauntered over to me. "Don't you like my body all slicked up with baby oil for you?"

"Yeah, I like," I panted as he straddled my lap. Instantly, I was hard as a rock as I reached around him and filled my hands with his firm ass. "I fucking love it, to be exact. But I demand for my love slave to show off his new garment."

"As my master commands it," Jared purred as he leaned forward and licked my bottom lip in a sign of submission. I moaned loudly as he moved off of my lap and slowly turned in a circle.

"Stop," I ordered when he was facing away from me. "Bend over, love slave."

"Oh shit," Cameron groaned as he started to strip. "This is the best fucking bet ever."

"I'll remember you said that when it's your turn." Jared snickered as he spread his legs wider and touched his toes. His tight ass was on perfect display, along with all the firm muscles in his legs and lower back. I knew there was a pretty pink little hole just waiting to be claimed under the black satin strip of the thong.

"Can we start now?" Rhyce whimpered as he yanked off his jeans. "We've all been celibate for weeks for fuck sake."

"Yes," I hissed as I kneeled behind Jared and pulled the thong to the side. I licked his hole several times, getting a loud groan from my mate in response.

"I can't stay in this position," Jared moaned.

"On the bed, hands and knees," I ordered as we both stood back up. He hurried to comply with my request as I got naked. "Cameron, use that evil tongue of yours on his ass."

"Gladly," Cameron purred and moved behind our hot, slicked up Alpha. Seconds later, we were all naked and on the bed.

"Will you stretch me out, my mate?" I asked Rhyce who smiled wickedly at me. "I want Cameron to ride Jared while I fuck him, with you inside me."

"Oh fuck, I'm gonna blow just from the visual," Jared panted as Cameron grunted his approval. After that it was a rush to get everyone ready. No one was sweet and tender, slowly preparing and having foreplay. We'd all been without too long. Cameron kept at Jared as I stretched out Cameron's ass, while Rhyce did mine.

"On your back, ass by the edge of the bed," I said to Jared as we were finally ready. He moved into position as Cameron straddled his cock.

"Give me the green light, baby," Cameron begged, and I smacked his ass hard.

"Impale yourself on his big cock," I growled. He did just that as I moaned and squeezed the base of my dick so I didn't come yet. When

Cameron was all the way seated on Jared, I moved in between Jared legs and lined up with his hole. I glanced down at our Alpha over Cameron's shoulder. "Are you ready for me, my mate?"

"Yes, god yes, stick that fucking pole in me," Jared whimpered. I smiled as I started to pushed into his tight virgin ass. "Oh shit, it burns so good."

"That's it, take my Omega cock into your Alpha ass," I groaned, feeling way too dominant and possessive. I went as slowly as I could even though Jared's ass seemed to suck me right in as if begging for my cock as much as he was.

"My turn," Rhyce growled once I was balls deep in Jared. I pushed Cameron forward and leaned over him as I pulled the cheeks of my ass apart for Rhyce. "So pretty, baby. Such a nice firm ass."

"And tight after no sex for so long," I moaned as he thrust forward. "Oh fuck, Rhyce. Shove it into me, I need to feel you."

"Gladly," he hissed as he pushed hard and bottomed out inside of me. We all stayed joined together for a minute, no one moving as we reveled in the feeling of all coming together for the first time.

"Fuck me good, Rhyce," I begged after I couldn't not move any longer. He licked his mating mark as he pulled back out before thrusting right back into me hard. His thrust caused me to push into Jared as Cameron moved off of his cock.

"Oh shit, I'm going to blow already," Jared moaned as his head thrashed on the bed. "I get to bottom always now that I'm the smallest."

"No way, you're too good at topping to always bottom," I said firmly as we started to move faster together as if one body. "I love the feel of you pounding into me, Jared."

"Good point, I do love fucking my baby," he grunted as he reached up and grabbed Cameron's cock. "You going to paint my chest?"

"You better believe it," Cameron panted. I moved Jared's legs further apart, changing the angle of my thrusts, and he cried out in pleasure. "Shit, I might want to always bottom, too."

"Okay, I get to try it next." Rhyce groaned as he licked my mating bite again.

"Tristan, you're going to bite me, right?" Cameron said as he rode Jared like a wild animal. "I want you to sink your teeth into me."

"After you bite me," Jared whimpered. "I want my other mates to mark me too."

"Oh fuck yeah," Cameron growled as he leaned over. I had a front row seat to it all. Rhyce was pounding into me so hard as I fucked Jared, the dual sensations of taking someone while being taken were driving me insane.

"Cameron," Jared cried out as our mate drank from him. The sight was so erotic that I couldn't help but wonder if that's what I looked like when they'd bit me.

"Fuck, Jared," I groaned as the muscles in his ass clamped down on my cock. Cameron must have gotten the idea because he lifted his head from Jared's throat and leaned back against me. I licked his neck before sinking my elongated canines into him.

"I love you, Tristan," Cameron yelled as he shot ropes of cum all over Jared's chest. It was enough to push me over the edge with Jared's muscles still convulsing around my cock. I roared out my release as I lifted my head from his neck. I loved the feeling of my seed pumping into my mate's ass, completing my first time giving instead of receiving.

"Holy shit," Rhyce cried out as my orgasm was rolling over me in waves. Seconds later I felt his cum fill my ass as he kept pumping into me. Cameron collapsed on Jared, and I wasn't far behind. I braced my weight on my arms as Rhyce gave one last hard thrust into my ass. "That was so worth waiting weeks for."

"It was worth waiting a lifetime for," I panted and then moaned as he pulled out of me. "I love you all so much."

"We love you, too, baby," Rhyce said, kissing my neck before collapsing on the bed next to Jared. Cameron groaned as he moved off of our Alpha and fell to the other side.

"I've never been so glad I like football," Jared whispered as he smiled up at me with tears shining in his eyes. "And that I saw the most beautiful creature at the Green Bay Packers game."

"I'm glad you saw me, and not just an Omega," I said as I leaned over and kissed him. "You saw me, Tristan, and I'll love you until the day I die, Jared."

"I don't deserve it, but I'll gladly accept it, baby," he replied, moaning as I pulled out of him. We all crawled up to the head of the bed, the four of us wrapped around each other.

"We really should, like, clean up or we're going to end up all sticking to each other." Rhyce snickered as he threw a leg over my hip. He was spooned behind me as I lay on my side over Jared, Cameron doing the same on the other side.

"We're sticking together no matter what," Cameron said firmly as he glanced between each of us. "No matter what, this is it, we're together always. No more bonehead moves, keeping our mouths shut when we shouldn't, or assuming the worst of each other. We're a family, and families don't do that when they love each other."

"I couldn't agree more, my mate," I replied, smiling widely at him as Jared and Rhyce agreed. And I knew with perfect certainty that we would be just fine and love each other for the rest of our days. It didn't hurt that I could also feel the love and happiness coming off of my men of course, but I'd just keep that to myself.

# THE END

**www.joyeeflynn.com**

# ABOUT THE AUTHOR

Joyee Flynn grew up in Chicago living in the same house all her life until she left for college. She loves to get lost in fantasy that only books could bring. She kept writing, short stories, romance, mystical, and of course adding in hot cowboys any chance she could. Her wide interest in reading was reflected in her writings. Currently Joyee lives with her dog, Marius, named after a vampire from Ann Rice's *Interview with the Vampire* series. She dreams of one day living out in Montana, enough land to have a few horses, and find a couple of cowboys of her own.

A lover of men, Joyee's all about them in any form in her books. Vampire, werewolf, military, doesn't matter at all as long as they are hot, hard, and sex fiends!

## *Also by Joyee Flynn*

Ménage Amour: North American Dragon 1: *Dragon Mine*
Ménage Amour: North American Dragon 2: *Dragon Ours*
Siren Classic: Marius Brothers 1: *Micah*
Siren Classic: Marius Brothers 2*: Remus*
Siren Classic: Marius Brothers 3: *Stefan*
Siren Classic: Marius Brothers 4: *Victor*
Ménage Amour: The O'Hagan Way 1: *A Dillon Sandwich*
Ménage Amour: The O'Hagan Way 2: *A Caleb Footlong*
Ménage Amour: Purrfect Mates 1: *Here Kitty, Kitty*
Ménage Amour: Purrfect Mates 2: *My Little Kitty*
Ménage Amour: Purrfect Mates 3: *Our Sexy Tiger*
Siren Classic: Hiding Hounds 1: *Sheriff Found*
Siren Classic: Sons of Thanatus 1: *My Maven, My Everything*

## *Also by Stormy Glenn and Joyee Flynn*

Ménage Amour: Delta Wolf 1: *Chameleon Wolf*
Ménage Amour: Delta Wolf 2: *Mating Games*
Ménage Amour: Delta Wolf 3: *Blood Lust*

Available at
**BOOKSTRAND.COM**

**Siren Publishing, Inc.**
**www.SirenPublishing.com**

CPSIA information can be obtained at www.ICGtesting.com

262441BV00005B/27/P

9 781610 345002